FUTURE DREAMS AND NIGHTMARES

DONALD FIRESMITH

Future Dreams and Nightmares

By Donald Firesmith

Copyright 2023 by Donald G. Firesmith

First Edition: May 2023

10 9 8 7 6 5 4 3 2 1

This book is a work of fiction. Any similarities to real people, living or dead, are purely coincidental. All characters and events in this work are figments of the author's imagination.

1. Science Fiction 2. Horror

Purchase autographed books by contacting the author at:

Magical Wand Press

20 Bradford Avenue

Pittsburgh, PA 15205

https://donaldfiresmith.com

Edited using Grammarly™, and ProWritingAid™

Book cover by Natasja Hellenthal (Beyond Book Covers).

Interior design by Donald Firesmith

Praise for Future Dreams and Nightmares

Midwest Book Review

"Get ready to dive into a world of alternate realities with this collection of short stories. Each tale in this captivating collection introduces you to new characters and takes you on a thrilling journey that will leave you craving more.

These thrilling stories will keep you on the edge of your seat. Look no further than this book, which is sure to captivate and excite you with its many twists and turns. Each story in this book presents a strong and compelling offering, delivering a unique and unforgettable reading experience.

Future Dreams and Nightmares is for those that are looking for a break from the mundane or simply want to immerse yourself in a world of excitement and adventure; this book has something for everyone.

Donald Firesmith has an innate gift for storytelling with his impeccable writing style. From thrilling adventures to thought-provoking mysteries, his words have the power to captivate and ignite your imagination. Whether you are a fan of fantasy, science fiction, or suspense, this collection offers something for every reader."

Booksshelf.com

"Firesmith's visionary tales infuse timeless themes with renewed energy... This compilation offers a swift journey. I assure you, choosing this adventure is a decision you won't regret."

Amy's Bookshelf Reviews

"I am a huge fan of Donald Firesmith. Whatever he writes, I know, without expectation, that it's going to be interesting, and very intriguing. Some of the stories reminded me of the Twilight Zone television show (yes, I watched the reruns), but it also reminded me of something I watched recently, which was Stephen King's collection of Nightmares and Dreamscapes. Yes, the stories are that good. I don't know what inspires Firesmith, but I'm glad he shares his intriguing and magnificent stories with readers. I am always honored to read his work. The author weaves a tangled web of stories and captures the reader. Future Dreams and Nightmares is a definite recommendation by Amy's Bookshelf Reviews."

The Avid Reader

"What an interesting set of short stories *Future Dreams and Nightmares* has. Each one will keep you guessing and a whole lot to think about. There is plenty of suspense and mystery to keep them interesting and very intriguing. Each will blow your mind in many different ways. Each is a blast to read."

TABLE OF CONTENTS

Memories	1
Mind Trap	11
A Mind Full of Memories	21
Everlife	32
Original Equipment	56
A Jump Too Far	60
We Service All	106
Close Encounters of the Fourth Kind	122
History is Written	173
Arianna	180
To Serve and Protect	191

MEMORIES

One wall displayed a beautiful mountain lake, while Clair de Lune played softly as the middle-aged man entered the waiting room at the Tranquility memory-deletion clinic. A gentle breeze blew ripples across the lake's surface, and the yellow leaves of the aspens fluttered like a million butterfly wings.

"Good morning, Mr. Harding," a disembodied woman's voice said. "Please take a seat. The doctor will see you shortly."

Sam Harding sat down on a comfortable couch in front of the display wall and tried to relax. Taking a deep breath, Sam willed the muscles in his neck and shoulders to loosen, but the decades-old tightness remained.

For most people suffering from post-traumatic stress disorder, their medical insurance pays for deleting their debilitating memories. Universal Healthcare would cover the cost if you didn't have insurance and were a wounded soldier, an accident victim, or the victim of a physical assault. But as a felon convicted of violent crimes, Sam had to pay the entire amount himself, and it had taken twelve long years for him to save enough for just a single treatment.

Future Dreams and Nightmares

Sam tapped his fingers nervously on the couch. What if the therapy didn't work? What if he needed more than one treatment? What if his horrendous flashbacks and nightmares continued?

Then Sam wondered how many of his victims had needed Tranquility's treatments to erase the devastating memories of what he had done. Addicted to the powerful street drug known as Craze, Sam had initially turned to burglary and armed robbery to pay for the increasingly frequent fixes he required to keep his inner demons at bay. But eventually, he lost control. He became a serial rapist who took his self-loathing out on the women he robbed while crazed on the highly addictive drug. Taking ever greater chances as his addiction sent him into a vicious spiral of highs and lows, the police inevitably identified and arrested him.

The judge sentenced Sam to twenty years without the possibility of parole. His first year — during which withdrawal often sent him to the prison hospital — seemed to last forever. Later, years of individual and group therapy forced him to face the terrible suffering he had brought on himself, his family, his friends, and, most of all, his many victims.

For the last twenty-nine years, Sam had been clean. And for each of those years, the memories of the pain he had caused ate at him. He had served his time and turned his life around. His parole board had decreed he was no longer a danger to himself or others. He had paid his debt to society, and today, the awful memories of what he did would finally be erased forever.

"Mr. Harding," the disembodied voice said, "the doctor will see you now."

A door silently swung open, and a nurse dressed in white said, "If you will follow me, please, I'll take you back now."

She led Sam to a room where a comfortable recliner sat waiting for him. To its left stood EKG and functional EEG displays to enable the doctor to monitor his heart and the functioning of various parts of his brain. To its right, an IV bottle hung from its metal stand.

"Please sit down. Once I hook you up and insert an IV line for the medications, I'll get your doctor."

The nurse began by attaching the EKG leads to Sam's chest, arms, and legs. Then she placed a tight-fitting, sensor-laden cap over his scalp. A 3D image of Sam's brain appeared on the second display, its lobes and internal components glowing like so many colorful ghosts in the machine of his mind. Twinkling clouds of tiny sparks showed the activity of his brain. The nurse finished by sliding the IV needle into the vein on the back of his hand with practiced ease.

"Now sit back and relax while I let your doctor know you're ready."

Future Dreams and Nightmares

Once again, Sam tried to relax. He closed his eyes and tried to concentrate on the soothing music that had followed him in from the waiting room.

A woman in her mid-forties briefly knocked on the door and entered. "Good afternoon, Mr. Harding," she said as she glanced at the monitors and IV. "I see my assistant has you properly prepped for the procedure. How are you feeling today?"

"Okay, I guess. A bit nervous you might accidentally erase memories I don't want to lose, but more worried that you won't delete all my terrible memories."

"Don't worry, Mr. Harding. Such concerns are only natural, but I assure you that you are in expert hands. Here at Tranquility, we've helped hundreds of patients delete their worst memories. Are you ready?"

"Doctor, I'm more than ready. I've been waiting and saving my money a very long time for this day."

"Okay, then, let's get started. Your memories are stored as engrams — neural circuits composed of neurons connected by synapses. The engrams are largely located in your brain's hippocampus and neocortex. But those associated with powerful emotions, such as fear and anger, also run through your brain's amygdalae."

Sam ignored the medical jargon, hoping she would get to the point.

Memories

"So, the first thing we will do is identify and chemically mark the synapses associated with the specific engrams you wish to delete. Then, I'll inject a second chemical that will permanently change those synapses, weakening the neural circuits that elicit those memories. When we're done, it will be as if the memories had never existed."

"That sounds wonderful, doctor. You have no idea how much that means to me."

The doctor smiled. "Of course, I do, Mr. Harding. I assure you, the results will be truly life-altering."

She picked up a needle and inserted it into the IV line, just a few inches from where it fed into Sam's vein.

"Okay, Mr. Harding, close your eyes. I want you to concentrate on the memories you wish to forget. Picture them clearly in your mind. Remember everything you can about the experiences: where you were, who you were with, what was said and done, and how you felt. Try to remember everything about them. Then, when you're ready, I want you to nod your head."

Sam closed his eyes and nodded a few seconds later.

The doctor injected the contents of the needle into the IV. "Keep remembering. Concentrate on each experience and try to picture it as clearly as you can."

Sam tried his best to remember each robbery, each assault, and each rape. He tried to recall his victims, their screams, and how they begged for mercy. But most of his memories were vague, distorted, and blurred by the countless doses of craze he had taken. The memories were like his terrible flashbacks and nightmares. Still, he kept at it, desperate to remember every single memory he wanted the doctor to erase.

"Okay, Mr. Harding. You may stop now and open your eyes."

Sam sighed and looked up at the doctor, who smiled back at him.

"The drug we used to mark the memories to be deleted only lasts a few minutes. Your other memories are safe now that your liver has metabolized it." She picked up a second needle and injected its contents into the IV line.

"So that's the drug that erases the memories," Sam guessed.

"Not quite, Mr. Harding." She paused and stared intensely into his eyes. "You don't remember me, do you?"

"Remember you?" Sam felt a strange sensation in his hands and feet that rapidly spread. "Hey, my arms, my legs... I can't move my arms and legs! What's going on?" Although wide awake, Sam couldn't move, and his voice had become a faint whisper.

Memories

The doctor smiled. "That's merely the effects of the powerful muscle relaxant I just gave you. I can't have you getting up or calling for help now, can I?"

Confused and increasingly afraid, Sam stared at the doctor. "Why are you doing this?" he breathed.

"You may not remember me, Mr. Harding, but I most definitely remember you. When I noticed your name on the patient schedule, I had to read your intake file to be sure. And once I saw your photo, I knew it was really you. After that, ensuring they assigned your treatment to me as my last patient of the day was easy. Soon, you and I will be the only ones in the building."

The doctor stared down at Sam. Her smile didn't reach her eyes.

"Help! Help!" Sam tried to shout, but his cries were barely audible.

"You still don't remember me?" The doctor sighed. "How disappointing. We met nearly thirty years ago when I was a graduate student studying for my doctorate in neurobiology. I was asleep, all alone in my apartment, when a noise woke me. When *you* woke me, Mr. Harding! You tied me up, and after rifling through my purse, you ransacked my apartment. You took my money and credit cards, but that wasn't enough for you. You beat me, and then you raped me! And once you'd finished, you beat me again! When I woke up three days later in the hospital, I had a concussion, two missing teeth, a broken nose, and three cracked ribs."

"I'm sorry," Sam whispered.

"Sorry? Do you actually think I care whether you're sorry, you sack of shit?" she shouted. Then she paused, took a deep breath, and felt her white-hot rage turn icy cold. "I could have had the hellish memories you burned into my brain erased. But some memories are just far too important to delete. My memories of what you did to me could have broken me, but instead, they made me strong. They gave me the drive to donate my services to any victim too poor to afford them. Because of you, I've treated dozens of women who otherwise would never have had their memories erased."

She turned, picked up the third needle, and stared at it. "But I have a different gift for you. Ordinarily, I would inject a drug to permanently weaken your marked synapses. But this needle contains a drug that will permanently strengthen those synapses. In fact, it will reinforce them to such a degree that the nerves comprising the marked engrams will constantly fire. In other words, Mr. Harding, the rest of your miserable life will consist of nothing but you reliving the terrible memories you wanted to delete. They will repeat, over and over again, never stopping long enough for you to have another thought, another experience. They never should have let you out of prison, Mr. Harding, so I'm sending you back. Only

Memories

this time, your prison will be your brain, and you will never be paroled."

Sam tried to scream as the doctor injected the third drug into his IV. But he barely made a sound as his eyes stared at her in horror.

...

Just after midnight, the police discovered the former craze addict lying in a fetal position in a garbage-strewn alley in a seedier part of town. With his eyes staring blankly and every muscle tightly clinched, they initially thought Sam Harding was dead and that rigor mortis had set in. But once they noticed his rapid shallow breathing, they requested an ambulance, which transported him to the inner-city's main hospital.

The emergency department doctors could do little for their patient. They prescribed beta blockers to slow his racing heart and muscle relaxants to treat his muscle spasms. But they could neither wake him nor determine the cause of his condition. They admitted him and eventually diagnosed him as suffering from an incurable idiopathic seizure.

Sam Harding was still unresponsive when they transferred him to a state-run nursing home one month later. And he spent the rest of his life there, trapped in a never-ending nightmare.

The staff soon learned to avoid his room. The horrendous expression of terror frozen on his face was more than any of them could stand.

AUTHOR'S COMMENTS

Who among us hasn't had terrible memories they would like to permanently delete from their memories? Yet, the pain of these memories often acts as a reminder for us to avoid the behaviors that initially led to them. Perhaps some memories just aren't meant to be forgotten.

MIND TRAP

The call I had been dreading for over a decade finally arrived at 3:45 one Thursday afternoon. Jacob's butler called me, saying that our master had called for me to come up to the penthouse and say goodbye. Grabbing my medical bag — more from habit than any hope that my friend would let me use my skills to save his life — I took the private elevator up some 90 floors. I stepped out into the home of Jacob Anderson, one of the Oligarchs who ruled the Solar System and the greatest philanthropist of the last hundred years. The view of Central City from the floor-to-ceiling windows was breathtaking, but I ignored it as I rushed to the master bedroom.

The two bodyguards at the door stepped aside, and the doors parted, granting me entry into the master's sanctum sanctorum, where he had been confined for the last eleven years. They closed and locked the doors behind me.

"Greetings, Simon," he said. His voice, once strong and commanding, was little more than a whisper. "I'm glad you're here with me as I leave on life's last grand adventure."

"Jacob, there is still time," I replied, shocked at how much his health had deteriorated since I had seen him just three days earlier. His skin had a bluish tint, and the whites of his eyes were distinctly yellow.

Future Dreams and Nightmares

Even under his blanket, I could see the swelling of his abdomen and lower extremities. Clearly, the medicines I had given him to combat his symptoms of multiple organ failure were failing to work.

"I could scan you into a mind vault in less than ten minutes and have you into one of your clones before dinner time. Then, you could be young and healthy again."

"Simon, you know I vowed to never use that technology again."

Mr. Anderson played a pivotal role in developing mind transfer technology well over three hundred years ago. And like the other Oligarchs, he had used it several times to greatly extend his life. But ever since an assassination attempt resulted in the murder of his wife and his previous physician some forty years ago, he had mysteriously refused to transfer into the body of a young and healthy clone. Soon after the attack, he hired me as his personal doctor, and I eventually became his closest friend.

"But why, Jacob?" I asked, frustrated by the dying man's cursed stubbornness. "Why? There is so much good you could still do."

"I know, Simon, God knows I know. But we all must atone for our sins. Even me."

"What are you talking about? I can't think of anyone who has done more for the citizens of Earth, the Moon, and Mars. You have funded countless

Mind Trap

public museums, amusement centers, and parks. You've also greatly improved your employees' working conditions, given them more than adequate wages, and provided them with free housing and healthcare. And you've lobbied the other Oligarchs to follow your example. Hell, you've done far more than all of them combined. But with you gone, there won't be anyone to protect the citizens from their exploitation. Things will revert to the way they were before..."

I paused, afraid I had crossed an uncrossable line. Before Jacob's wife was murdered, he had been one of the worst of the Oligarchs: greedy and ruthless, murdering with impunity as he climbed to the top over the ruins of other mid-level Oligarchs. Like the others, he had treated his employees as slaves to use and abuse as he saw fit. Mentioning that period of his life had resulted in the firing or disappearance of more than one member of Jacob's staff.

"I'm sorry, sir. I meant no offense."

"Don't worry, Simon. I'm not offended. Facing one's imminent death has allowed me to put things into perspective. Which reminds me of why I called you here, even though I still won't let you transfer me into a new clone."

I waited expectantly while Jacob paused to catch his breath. He closed his eyes.

"You were saying," I coaxed.

Future Dreams and Nightmares

"I know this must be frustrating to you, me not letting you save me. But I felt that after all this time, I owed you an explanation. It's too late now for my secret to hurt me, and I need someone to do one last job for me, a job I can no longer do myself. So, I ask you, Simon, will you grant me one last wish?"

"Of course, Jacob. Anything."

"Okay, grab a chair and sit down. I'm going to tell you a secret, one that is known to only two others. And it is a secret that none of you can ever tell."

I took the chair from his desk and sat down close enough to hold his hand when the time came.

"As you know, I used to be like all the other Oligarchs. I had extensive holdings not only on Earth but also on the Moon, Mars, and several of the larger asteroids."

I nodded. Everyone who interacted with Oligarchs knew that much.

"To maintain control of my many businesses, I often needed to visit my properties, factories, and other facilities. That naturally meant uploading my mind into a mind vault, having the associated software and data radioed to one of my off-planet facilities, and having it downloaded into either one of my clones on Mars or the Moon or into a more robust robotic body out in the Belt. Then, once I was done, I would have my clone or robot placed back into storage and have my mind radioed back and transferred into my sleeping body."

So far, that was precisely how the other Oligarchs managed their holdings. Given their insatiable desire for power and unwillingness to share it with even their own clones, it was no wonder that the Oligarchs only permitted their minds to reside in one body or vault at a time. I wondered when Jacob would tell me something that wasn't common knowledge.

"Back in those days," he continued, "I did whatever I wanted. I treated my employees as little more than easily replaceable slaves. I drank, partied, and had more mistresses than I could remember. And I didn't care who knew or who I hurt. I figured that to keep the lifestyle I'd given her, Lilith would put up with anything I did. So I made sure she knew I'd cut her off the second she betrayed me with another man."

I suspected as much, given the public behavior of the other Oligarchs.

"Anyway, I hadn't realized just how much I'd hurt her and, more importantly, just how far she'd go to get her revenge. I didn't know Robert Franklin, a relatively poor but ambitious fourth son of a mid-level Oligarch, had seduced her. Knowing that he would never inherit his father's wealth, Franklin devised a scheme to delete my mind once it arrived back on Earth and have his own mind downloaded into my body. That way, he could steal my identity, take over my business empire, and live my life with my wife."

Now, that was totally unexpected. Not only was it utterly inconsistent with the official story of what happened, it was also very challenging technically and highly illegal to upload one person's mind into another person's body or clone.

"There was only one problem Franklin and Lilith had to solve. Neither of them knew how to use the mind transfer equipment, so they needed an accomplice to do their dirty work. Specifically, they needed your predecessor, Dr. Jonathon Schwan, to do the actual mind transfer. So first, needing a reason for the doctor to go along with their scheme, Franklin talked my wife into seducing him. Then, keeping Franklin's existence a secret, Lilith would convince my doctor that she loved him and that they could share my wealth and power once he deleted me, and the doctor downloaded himself into my body. But Dr. Schwan didn't know they intended to kill him once he had set up the transfer, so that Franklin could be downloaded into my body instead.

"It took a while, but Lilith could be very persuasive and persistent. She convinced Dr. Schwan that I deserved to die, and eventually, the doctor agreed to kill me and take my place."

Jacob paused again to catch his breath. "Lilith and Franklin nearly managed to pull off their plan. But, unfortunately for them, Doctor Schwan overheard my wife bragging to Franklin about how she had totally fooled him."

Once more, Jacob had to pause to catch his breath. This time, it took a little longer before he could continue. "Realizing Franklin meant to kill him, Doctor Schwan drugged my darling wife and uploaded her mind into a mind vault. Then the doctor took one of my guns and shot and killed her body. When Franklin arrived, the doctor also killed him with the same gun. With my wife's body and Franklin dead, the doctor was alone and ready for me when the radio transmission containing my mind arrived back from Mars."

"But I don't understand," I said. "If that's what happened, how did you survive and kill Dr. Schwan? And what happened to the mind vault holding your wife's mind?"

"How indeed," Jacob said. "Simon, now we come to the core of my secret. Dr. Schwan uploaded Jacob Anderson's mind into a second vault and then downloaded his own mind into Anderson's waiting body."

"But that means you're not Jacob Anderson!" I exclaimed.

"Correct. I'm not really Jacob Anderson. I'm Dr. Jonathon Schwan. Having killed Franklin and uploaded Lilith's and Jacob Anderson's minds into mind vaults, I only had one more crime to commit.

Future Dreams and Nightmares

So, I took another of Anderson's guns and killed my old body.

"I called the police and told them there had been an assassination attempt. And when they arrived, I told them that Dr. Schwan had assassinated my wife and Franklin and that I had no choice but to kill the doctor before he killed me. As an Oligarch, the police knew they had to believe my lies. Besides, finding the doctor's fingerprints and DNA on the gun that killed Franklin and Lilith would corroborate my story."

"But what happened to Jacob and Lilith? What did you do with the vaults that you uploaded their minds into? Did you kill them, too?"

"God, no." Dr. Schwan chuckled. "They each deserved a much more fitting punishment for their sins. Now, will you keep your word and do one last thing for me?"

"Yes," I answered, dreading what the man I thought I knew would ask of me. But I had given my word to a friend I had known for decades. I had promised the greatest philanthropist of the era that I would grant his dying wish.

"Simon, do you see that box over on the mantle?"

"Yes," I answered nervously.

"Bring it over. I need to press my thumb on the sensor on top to unlock it."

With increasing dread, I did as the old man asked.

Once the sensor verified my friend's identity as Jacob Anderson, the lid popped open. Inside were two mind vaults wired together and also wired to the box.

"You are holding Jacob and Lilith Anderson in your hands," my friend continued. "I've had them wired together so that they could never get away from each other and only have each other to torment. I also wired them to a microphone and camera hidden in the front of the box. Thus, I had forced them to observe me living Jacob's life, liquidating his empire to undo as much as possible of the damage and injustice that he and the other Oligarchs had done. I imagine that after fifty years, the pair are probably quite incurably insane."

"Oh my God," I whispered, realizing the extent and magnitude of the living hell Dr. Schwan had put them through.

"Now, hold the box up in front of me."

With trembling hands, I did as he told me.

"Jacob and Lilith," he said, staring straight into the box's camera. "By unlocking the box, I started a five-minute timer. I had it programmed so that you, and only you, can hear it counting down. When it reaches zero, an electrical surge will fry the circuitry of your mind vaults. So, you see, I'm finally setting you two free. All three of us are dying today."

A few minutes later, I heard a faint buzzing, and thin streams of smoke rose from the mind vaults. That was when the terrible realization hit me. Although I was a doctor trained to save lives, I had just participated in a double murder! But then I convinced myself that their death was justified and actually a blessing that released them from their hellish prison. I spent the rest of the afternoon and evening sitting with my old friend, and I held his hand as he peacefully drifted away.

AUTHOR'S COMMENTS

The ability to download one's mind into a cloned or robotic body is a frequent science fiction trope. So, I thought it interesting to consider how such a transfer could go wrong or be misused.

A MIND FULL OF MEMORIES

He awoke to the soft sounds of the nearby babbling brook and the chirping of a pair of robins in the Douglas firs surrounding their campsite. Sarah lay next to him, and the inviting warmth of her body tempted him to stay in the sleeping bags they had zipped together. *Just ten more minutes,* he thought. *Then I'll get up.*

He smiled, remembering how they had made love the night before. *Sarah's wonderful,* he thought. *She's beautiful, smart, and kind. She could have had anyone, but she chose me. I've got to be the luckiest man alive.* Gently, so as not to wake her, he rolled towards her. Their bodies fit together as though meant for one another.

She awoke, sighed, and wiggled to press her hips against him, causing him to realize he had a morning erection.

"Mmmm," she purred. "My, you're up early this morning. I'd have thought last night was enough to keep you satisfied for more than a few hours."

"I can never get enough of you," he replied and then sighed, realizing he had to pee. "Unfortunately, nature calls."

"Me, too," she said with regret. "Come on. Let's get up. We still have another fourteen miles to go before we reach Crystal Lake. The wait will give you something to look forward to tonight."

Reluctantly climbing out of their sleeping bags, they put on their clothes that the crisp mountain air had made freezing cold. Then, after a quick breakfast of oatmeal cooked over an open campfire, they packed their stuff in their backpacks and headed up the trail that followed the stream up to its source at the lake.

With the sun shining down from a cloudless sky, the solitude of an empty trail beyond the reach of day hikers, and the woman he loved, the day was perfect. John's life was perfect, and he wouldn't exchange it for the world.

...

Mr. Henderson, the Shady Grove county-run nursing home's administrator, ushered the neurosurgeon into one of the facility's single-patient rooms. Smelling of stale urine and disinfectant, it was empty of any personal possessions or items visitors might have left. "This is the patient I told you about," the administrator said, pointing to a man lying motionless in the bed, staring blindly up at the ceiling.

Dr. Anderson picked up the patient's chart hanging from the end of the bed. "John Miller, age 32. What can you tell me about him?"

A Mind Full of Memories

"It's a tragic case," Mr. Henderson replied. "Eight years ago, Mr. Miller was a healthy young man just out of college with a bright future ahead of him. Then he had the misfortune of being in a convenience store when he saw a man accosting a young woman. Mr. Miller came to her aid, and the two men exchanged angry words."

The administrator sighed. "The man stormed out of the store, only to return a minute later with a gun. He shot Mr. Miller twice. One bullet struck him in the back of his head, severely damaging his visual cortex. The second bullet hit his lower back, severing his spinal cord. The injuries left him largely blind, in a coma, and paralyzed from the waist down. For the first few years, his fiancée would occasionally visit, but he's had no visitors since then."

Dr. Anderson leaned over the bed. "Can you hear me, Mr. Miller?" he said, raising his voice. The patient gave no sign he was aware of the men in his room. Dr. Anderson pressed against the nail bed of the patient's index finger, but the man showed no reaction to what would ordinarily be a painful stimulus. "How long has he been like this?" the doctor asked.

"Mr. Miller was in a coma for the first five years and has been in a minimally conscious state for the last six. Most of the time, he's totally unresponsive, but he occasionally responds to simple commands, such as squeezing your finger. Unfortunately, he also suffers from frequent, long-lasting bouts of lateral temporal lobe epilepsy."

Dr. Anderson looked back at the patient's chart. According to the man's medical record, he had seizures that were limited to his right temporal lobe. He had some twenty such focal seizures a day, each lasting up to an hour. Because their only visible symptoms were changes to his breathing and an increased heart rate, electroencephalograms (EEGs) have been required to verify the diagnosis. In the first five years after Mr. Miller's shooting, his doctors had tried all the standard anticonvulsants. But they either were ineffective or had unacceptable side effects.

The administrator sighed. "Sadly, the only thing we can do for him is to keep him fed and hydrated, clean him when he soils himself, and turn him so that he doesn't get bedsores. I'm afraid we had basically given up on him and have just been waiting for him to die. But when I read about your work, I thought you might be able to give him a life worth living."

"I understand," Dr. Anderson said. "Well, I can localize and remove the brain tissue that causes Mr. Miller's epilepsy. And I can insert tiny electrodes into his posterior hypothalamus to stimulate him into wakefulness. But I will need an MRI of his

A Mind Full of Memories

brain to estimate how much of his vision he's lost, and we won't know for sure until we wake him up."

"That sounds wonderful," Mr. Henderson said. "I hate to think of him wasting away in here for another twenty or thirty years."

"Does Mr. Miller have any next of kin who can authorize his treatment?"

"No. His father died when he was a teenager, and cancer killed his mother a few years after the shooting. Before she passed, she begged us to cure her son, but until now, we've failed to honor her dying wish. Because he has no known relatives, the state has given us custody and the responsibility for making all medical decisions on his behalf."

"Excellent," Dr. Anderson said. "Obtaining informed consent for treatment is often very difficult when dealing with comatose patients."

"So, that means you'll take his case?"

"I will. I think we have a good chance of treating his epilepsy and waking Mr. Miller so he can get on with his life."

"Dr. Anderson, you're the first doctor in years to give me hope. I hate to raise the matter of cost, but the treatment you're describing is undoubtedly expensive. Most of our funding comes from the state and county. Spending so much on Mr. Miller naturally means that there will be less available for our other patients."

Future Dreams and Nightmares

"I wouldn't worry about that. I have sufficient research grants and foundation money to cover most of Mr. Miller's treatments. And those grants will enable me to waive my personal fees. What we learn from him will advance my research and hopefully enable us to improve the technology."

...

Although the night had left a thin layer of frost on the trees and bushes along the trail, the morning grew pleasantly warm as the couple hiked up the gorge toward Crystal Lake. Their only company was the occasional deer and the trout swimming in the creek's clear water. Although they talked off and on about their plans for the future, they mostly walked in silence, enjoying the quiet solitude of the forest that spread around them for miles in every direction. Their shared love of nature and the majestic wilderness of the Cascade Mountain Range only strengthened their love for each other. At times like this, were it not for the size of their student loans, he would gladly trade his job and apartment in the city for a small lakeside cabin and the life of a forest ranger with the woman he loved.

...

Two weeks later, the administrator had Mr. Miller transferred to the Cascade Institute's research hospital. Once the man was admitted, Dr. Anderson ordered a comprehensive set of brain scans, including functional magnetic resonance imaging, computed tomography, positron emission tomography, and single photon emission tomography. Using them, the doctor precisely pinpointed the lesion causing Mr. Miller's epilepsy and identified the correct location in his posterior hypothalamus where the doctor would place the stimulation electrodes that would wake his patient from his minimally conscious state. Finally, the doctor used the scans to determine the location and severity of the damage to Mr. Miller's visual cortex, enabling the neurosurgeon to predict that he would regain at least some of his vision.

Through all but one test, Mr. Miller seemed oblivious to everything happening around him. His only response occurred during the extremely loud fMRI scan, when his heart and breathing rate were elevated.

...

After a wonderful weekend spent together in the wilderness, the time had finally come for Sarah and her fiancé to come down from the mountains and return to their jobs in the city. But halfway down to the trailhead where they had parked their car, the sky grew overcast, and it began to rain. Soon, the light rain became a drenching downpour. Lightning split the sky, and deafening thunder boomed throughout the forest. They walked faster, but the trail grew muddy, and they had to slow down to minimize their risk of slipping and turning an ankle.

However, the storm eventually passed, and the sun broke through the clouds.

By the time the exhausted couple finally arrived at the trailhead's parking lot, their clothes were soaked, and their hiking boots were caked with mud. But that didn't matter. Their weekend alone in the mountains left them contented and refreshed. On the drive back to the city, they were already discussing which trail they would hike next and dreaming of the cabin they would one day build on the secluded shore of a remote lake.

...

Finally, the day of the surgery arrived. Once the nurses had prepped Mr. Miller and shaved and sterilized a patch of skin over his right temple, the operation began. Dr. Anderson started by making a C-shaped incision and folding back a flap of skin to reveal the white bone beneath. Then, after drilling a small hole in his patient's skull, he sliced through the three protective layers of the cerebral meninges to expose the man's brain. It pulsed slightly with each heartbeat. Then, it was a relatively simple matter for the surgeon to excise the marble-size lesion that was the source of his right temporal lobe epilepsy.

...

Tired from their hike, the couple retired to bed early. But they were young and in love. A goodnight kiss turned into a second, more passionate kiss. They had just begun making love when…

...

Using a fluoroscope to guide him, Dr. Anderson then inserted a thin endoscope through the same opening of the skull and gently pushed it into the brain until its end reached the posterior of his patient's hypothalamus. Satisfied that it was in the correct location, he withdrew the endoscope, leaving behind a tiny wire that would deliver a small voltage to the spot that controlled his patient's waking and alertness. Dr. Anderson then ran the wire under his patient's skin to a small neuro-stimulation device he had inserted through an incision he had made below Mr. Miller's collarbone.

With the device connected to the wire, the only thing left to do was to close the incisions and wait several hours for the general anesthesia to wear off.

...

Using a wireless remote, Dr. Anderson activated his patient's neuro-stimulation device. "Mr. Miller, can you hear me?"

There was no response.

The doctor increased the voltage sent into his patient's hypothalamus. "Mr. Miller, can you hear me?"

Future Dreams and Nightmares

The man moaned weakly and briefly opened his eyes before closing them again.

Dr. Anderson increased the voltage again. "Mr. Miller, wake up!"

The man in the bed opened his eyes. They darted around the room, trying to make sense of the blurry colors and shapes. "Sarah... Sarah, where are..." he whispered.

"Mr. Miller. My name is Dr. Anderson. You've been seriously injured and are in a hospital."

"Where's Sarah?"

"Who?"

"Sarah. Where's Sarah, my fiancé?"

"Mr. Miller, you've been in a coma for five years and then minimally conscious for another seven. I'm afraid your fiancé's not here."

"I want to see Sarah!"

"Mr. Miller, I'm sorry, but I don't know where Sarah is. It's been twelve years since your injury. I'm afraid she eventually stopped visiting you and moved on with her life."

"Nooooo! That's impossible. She was right here. We were just making love."

"I'm sorry, Mr. Miller, but what you remember were merely hallucinations caused by your temporal lobe epilepsy. But now that I've removed the lesion that caused your seizures, those hallucinations won't bother you anymore."

...

The hospital staff tried to help Mr. Miller come to terms with his near-total blindness, his inability to walk, let alone hike in his beloved mountains, and his lost love. They failed. Mr. Miller begged his doctors and nurses to throw away the neurostimulator that enabled him to be awake. But even when they let him sleep, his dreams and nightmares were no substitute for his seizures' vivid hallucinations. Mr. Miller died three weeks later from a broken heart.

On the other hand, Dr. Anderson considered his operation a complete success.

AUTHOR'S COMMENTS

Sometimes, healing a patient can violate a doctor's oath to do no harm. Just because a new technology becomes available does not mean that it right for everyone.

EVERLIFE

Alexis Huntington was asleep, and the jumbled images and sounds of her continuous series of dreams were overwhelming. In one dream, she was a little girl playing in her bedroom at her family's Long Island mansion. In another, she was sitting in a class at the private boarding school her parents sent her to as a teenager. Then, she was a grown woman, wandering the mansion's empty rooms after her parents died.

"Wake up, Alexis."

She opened her eyes to see her husband, John Philip Huntington II, leaning over her. The unexpected look of worry on his face confused her.

"What?" she whispered. Her voice was slurred, and when she tried to sit up, she could barely lift her head.

"Don't try to move yet. You'll feel better soon."

"But what's wrong?" she asked, still stubbornly trying to rise. Already, she was feeling stronger and managed to lift herself on her elbows. "Why am I so weak?"

"I'm afraid you've been in an accident," he answered.

"An accident?" Alexis repeated. "But I don't remember. Why can't I remember?"

Everlife

"It was a terrible car wreck. And you were injured."

"But I don't feel injured," she argued. "In fact, I'm feeling much better now. I don't hurt anywhere." Then she paused. "Was anyone else injured?"

"No, you were alone in the car," John paused as if searching for the right way to tell her. "Alexis, you were critically injured. I'm sorry, but I'm afraid you didn't survive."

"What?" she exclaimed, throwing back her covers and standing up. She staggered a bit, still weak on her feet, but pushed her husband away when he reached out to steady her. "What is this, some kind of sick joke? Why are you saying this?"

If only her mind weren't so fuzzy, making it nearly impossible for her to think clearly. Her husband pointed over her shoulder towards the door. She saw the family's private doctor and nurse silently standing there. Her doctor looked back at her and nodded. Alexis turned to the nurse, who also nodded in agreement.

"But I don't understand," she said, looking back at her husband. "If only I could remember." Then a memory slowly returned. She had been lying in a hospital bed with the recording helmet firmly attached to her head. She and John were at the Everlife resurrection complex having their memories scanned and recorded in case they ever needed to be revived. "Oh no," she whispered, sitting back on her bed.

"Thank goodness you convinced me to have our memories recorded," John said. "God knows it was expensive, even with your resurrection policy, but it was worth it. I thought I'd lost you. You can't imagine what I went through, seeing your former body after the wreck. It was terrible. But look at you now. Everlife did a great job with your clone. If I didn't know better, I'd swear the accident never happened."

So, this is my clone's body, she thought, looking down at herself. Strange that she didn't feel any different. Her brain fog was rapidly fading, enabling her to think more clearly. She remembered now that this was how the salesperson at Everlife had said it would be. Once they had downloaded her stored memories into her newly cloned body, there would be no physical difference. And since Congress passed the Resurrection Amendment to the Constitution, there was no legal difference either. So, she didn't just feel and think that she was Alexis Huntington; she *was* Alexis Huntington, with all her wealth and legal rights. Her former body was now nothing more than medical waste and replacement parts for those insufficiently wealthy to afford resurrection in a newly cloned body.

"How long has it been?" she asked, realizing that her husband looked only a little older than the day Everlife had recorded her memories. His hair was perhaps a little grayer and thinner, but nothing more.

"Since you were recorded? Nearly two years," he answered.

Two years, she thought. *Two years of memories that were now lost forever. I wonder what those two years were like. What I was like.*

John was the Chief Financial Officer of Quantum Infotech, a huge multinational conglomerate. Several hours later, after the doctor and nurse had left, her husband said, "I'm sorry, dear, but I have to go back to our corporate headquarters."

"Now?" she asked. "I've just been resurrected, and you're going to leave me?"

"I'm sorry, dear, but it can't be helped. I've already had to take off the last couple of days, and I'm in charge of our acquisition of a major AI computing company. Negotiations are in a very delicate state, and I've got to be there to close the deal."

"When will you be back?" Alexis asked. "I'll need to tell the cook when to prepare dinner."

"Not until late," he answered. "The entire team will work until at least midnight, maybe later. We'll have dinner catered, so have the cook fix your dinner whenever you're hungry."

How like him, she thought, angrily. Even after having just been revived from the dead, her husband couldn't take the time to be there for her. Even before her recording at Everlife, he'd become distant, not at all like the young, up-and-coming manager she had met and married so many years ago.

Over the next two days, Alexis barely saw her husband, and her resentment grew. He left early and worked until late at night, leaving the maid and cook as her only company in the otherwise empty mansion.

Alexis was sitting in front of the wall entertainment screen, trying to catch up with the two years of news she had missed since Everlife had recorded her memories when the maid came in.

"There's a Mr. Jason Morgan from the New Life Insurance Company to see you, ma'am. He says he needs to speak to you concerning your recent resurrection."

"Show him into the library and tell him I'll be in shortly," Alexis said, curious to learn why an insurance agent might want to talk with her. Still, as her husband had risen through the ranks of Quantum Infotech, she had taken over more and more of the family's financial affairs. She changed from her casual lounging gown into a more presentable dress and quickly checked her makeup before meeting the man in the library.

"Mr. Morgan," she said. "What can I do for you?"

"Mrs. Huntington, I'm an insurance fraud investigator with the New Life Insurance Company. I'd like to talk to you about our coverage of your recent resurrection."

"Fraud investigator?" she asked. "I was killed in a car accident, and my policy obviously paid to have me brought back to life. Isn't that exactly the eventuality that my policy should cover?"

"Yes, Ma'am, it is," he agreed. "However, I'd like to discuss an unusual aspect of your resurrection with you."

"Unusual? I died, and my policy with your company paid for my resurrection. That sounds straightforward to me."

"Well, I'm not sure how to tell you this, but this was actually your third resurrection in six months."

"What?" she exclaimed. "That's impossible! John would have told me if I'd been resurrected."

"I'm afraid not," he said, taking two folders out of his briefcase and handing them to her. "Here are our files for your first two resurrections."

Alexis quickly glanced through the documents. "This can't be right," she said, shaking her head in disbelief. "How can these papers be real?" She looked up at the fraud investigator. "How do I know this isn't part of some elaborate scheme to somehow, I don't know, scam me out of money?"

"I can easily prove it to you," he replied.

"How?"

Mr. Morgan took his phone out of his pocket. "Everlife gives every clone a tiny tattoo on the back of their neck just below the hairline that identifies the resurrection number. So, if you'll hold up your hair, I'll take a picture of yours."

Unconvinced, she nevertheless stood, turned her back, and lifted her hair out of the way. A few seconds later, he handed her his phone. The screen displayed an enlarged picture of her neck. She knew it was hers because she recognized the chain of her necklace. And just below her hairline, she saw a small black tattoo consisting of just three characters: EL3.

"Oh, my God! It's true." She couldn't understand it. Why had her husband not mentioned this to her?

Returning his phone to his pocket, Mr. Morgan continued. "Your New Life policy paid for your first resurrection when you broke your neck falling down the stairs. The inspection was essentially a formality. Mr. Huntington appeared to be a properly grieving husband, and there was no evidence of anything unusual. New Life paid for your resurrection, and the case was closed.

"After you drowned in a boating accident, your policy also paid for your second resurrection, but only once I'd investigated your death and found no conclusive evidence of fraud. While two covered deaths within months of each other are highly unlikely, they are not unheard of.

"When I was in the military, we had a saying: 'Once is happenstance, twice may be a coincidence, but three times is enemy action.' The probability of three accidental deaths, especially in such a short time, is so vanishingly small as to be unbelievable. Therefore, when we informed your husband that we would not cover your third resurrection without first performing an extensive investigation, he told us that to avoid the inconvenience, he would rather pay for the procedure himself. My management, therefore, canceled your policy and closed the books on your case."

"But you can't cancel my policy! I might need it again." Besides her simmering resentment and anger at her husband for ignoring her while she recovered from her resurrection, now he was keeping facts from her. Important facts! What other secrets could he be hiding?

"I'm afraid that we can, and we did. Your contract with New Life included an escape clause covering cancellation if the client does not permit our free access to data surrounding a client's death. That said, I suspected your drowning was no accident, but I couldn't find any evidence of foul play. Now, however, I'm convinced you've been the victim of attempted murder at least twice, maybe even three times."

"Attempted murder?" she asked, confused by his choice of words. "Since I died, don't you mean murder?"

"Unfortunately, New York State has not yet updated its laws concerning murder to take resurrection into account. Because you are still alive, technically, you can't have been murdered. Instead, the law views it as an attempted murder."

"But who could possibly want me dead? Surely, you're not saying that my husband tried to murder me."

"Mrs. Huntington, while I have my suspicions, I am not in the position to accuse anyone yet. The only real evidence we have is the implausible rarity of your deaths. That said, I would like to understand your husband's curious behavior. I have learned you inherited this mansion and a great deal of money upon the deaths of your parents. On the other hand, Mr. Huntington's income comes from his salary and bonuses as CFO of Quantum Infotech. While he undoubtedly earns a great deal, I suspect you are the source of most of your combined wealth."

"That is true," she admitted. "Do you suspect my husband of killing me for my money?"

Everlife

"Not at all, Mrs. Huntington. If he did, he wouldn't have paid to resurrect you. No, I suspect he might have another motive. Is it possible that you discovered something illegal or perhaps immoral, something that he would do anything to keep secret? Perhaps as the person responsible for a major multinational's finances, he has committed insider trading or embezzlement."

Alexis didn't know what to think. She wanted to trust her husband. But he was a proud man, and his parents were poor when he was growing up. She had occasionally suspected he'd found her family's great wealth intimidating. And she knew the acquisition of easy money could be a strong temptation.

"Mrs. Huntington, because a large percentage of women's murders are committed by their spouses, I have discreetly investigated your husband. I've learned that he regularly works very long hours and is rarely home in the evenings. How would you describe your relationship with him? Would you say that the two of you are close?"

She sighed. "Not as close as we once were. But I suppose that's not all that unusual for a couple when a man's job requires most of his time and attention."

"Mrs. Huntington, "I have observed that your husband often has a late dinner with a younger woman who also works at Quantum Infotech. And their behavior toward each other seems more than professional. I suspect that she and your husband are having an affair."

Confused, hurt, and angry, Alexis still had trouble believing her husband had a mistress. Surely, she thought, her love and willingness to cater to his needs had to be sufficient. "Mr. Morgan, I love my husband, and he loves me. I don't think he would ever break the law or have an affair." Yet even as she spoke those words, she realized they might be little more than wishful thinking.

"Alexis, that is exactly what you told me after your second death. But you were less sure each time we talked over the next three weeks. Eventually, you decided to confront your husband, and the following day, you were dead."

His sudden unexpected use of her first name surprised her. Had something developed between him and her second clone? His look of concern implied more than a mere professional interest in her safety. She also realized that the attractive man's attention and concern made her feel desirable in a way she hadn't felt for many years. If only her memory of the man hadn't died with her second clone.

"Mr. Morgan, what aren't you telling me?"

"That I'm not just interested in solving this case. Your second clone and I grew close during our short time together before she died. Alexis, I know you don't have her memories, but I can't help seeing you as the same person I was falling in love with. He's killed you twice, and now I'm terrified that he'll kill you again."

She saw the grief in his expression and heard the fear in his voice. "Oh," she said, staring closely at the man who was both a stranger and yet strangely something more. She sighed. "I'm not my second clone, Mr. Morgan, and I don't share any feelings she might have had for you. At least not yet."

"You're right, Alexis. It's unfair of me to assume anything else. But seeing you again, knowing you're in danger, I had to tell you how important you are to me."

"Understood. Anyway, I certainly won't develop such feelings if I die again, at least not unless I'm resurrected. For now, Mr. Morgan, my primary goal — *our* primary goal — must be to keep me alive. And to do that, we need to know for sure if it's John who's killing me and, if so, why."

"I agree. But we must have conclusive proof before we go to the police."

"I've always handled the family finances, so it will be easy for me to check John's credit cards and see what he's been spending his money on. Then, this evening, I'll send the staff home early so I'll have the house to myself. Once I'm alone, I'll be free to go through my husband's desk and see if I can get into the wall safe in his home office. He's a man of habit and probably hasn't changed his combination in years. Even if he has, I bet I can guess it. With any luck, I should also be able to guess his password so that I can log in on his computer and look for any sign of insider trading or embezzlement."

"Alexis, remember, I'm a fraud investigator. I have a lot of experience searching documents for evidence of crimes. I should stay here and help you because I'll probably be able to spot things you'd miss."

"No, Mr. Morgan. We can't risk having my husband discover you here. He expects me to be in the house, but you won't have an excuse to be alone with me in the evening. So instead, I want you to see if he's really working late at Quantum Infotech."

"Okay, Alexis, but for God's sake, be careful. Make sure you don't leave any physical or digital trace of what you're doing."

"Don't worry. I'll be careful. I'll make copies of anything I find and bring them to you."

"Okay," he answered. "Do you know the Jade Palace?"

"The little Asian restaurant on Fifth and Holbrook?"

"That's the one. It's not more than a quarter mile from here. You can meet me there and show me what you've found. Then we can decide what to do next."

"Okay. I'll call you when I'm on the way. In the meantime, you'd better go. I don't want the staff to be curious about how much time you're spending here and telling my husband."

"Okay, Alexis. I'll leave, but please check in with me so that I know you're safe."

"I will."

After Jason had left, Alexis logged onto her computer and began checking her husband's credit card accounts. However, none of the transactions appeared suspicious.

Then, after dinner, Alexis gave the maid and cook the evening off. And once they'd left, she got to work. She started by going through the drawers of her husband's desk. Next, she spent an hour reading various documents, many of which related to Quantum Infotech's acquisition of an AI software company. Once more, she found nothing suspicious, although she had to admit she didn't actually understand much of it.

Perhaps I should have let Mr. Morgan stay, she thought. *I really don't know enough about accounting to understand what I'm looking at.*

Future Dreams and Nightmares

Alexis had no more luck when she tried logging in on her husband's computer. She naturally couldn't use its fingerprint reader, so she tried logging in using passwords instead. However, none of her several dozen guesses were successful. *Damn! I thought for sure I knew John well enough to guess his password.*

Next, she removed the large painting that hid their wall safe. It took six guesses before she learned it was the day, month, and year of his hire date at Quantum Infotech. That's when she made her first discoveries.

The safe contained ten bundles of banknotes, each containing one hundred hundred-dollar bills. *So why the hell is John keeping $100,000 in cash in the safe?*

What Alexis found next was far more concerning: three passports, each with her husband's photograph, but a different name. "John, what the hell are you up to?" she whispered, shaking her head in disbelief.

Alexis also found a small black notebook, the contents of which were written in her husband's handwriting. Luckily, the first page held his computer password: the name Emma, followed by six digits that had to be a birthday. She had no idea who Emma was, only that she was some fifteen years younger than her and her husband. *Mr. Morgan was right*, she thought. *The bastard does have a mistress!* It also had the information and associated password on a credit card she didn't recognize, an exclusive American Express Platinum Card.

The next following pages of the notebook held three lists labeled Switzerland, The Cayman Islands, and Singapore. Entries on the lists consisted of the name of a bank, followed by one or more strings of digits. The implication seemed unmistakable. He had set up multiple secret numbered bank accounts.

The final unexpected item in the safe was a thumb drive that Alexis suspected held documentation of whatever financial crimes her husband was committing.

Alexis placed the bundles of cash, the three forged passports opened to show John's photographs and fake names, the notebook, and the thumb drive on his desk. Then she used her phone's camera to take photos of them. She also took pictures of the notebook's pages, documenting the numbered bank accounts.

Finally, Alexis used the computer password she'd found in the notebook to unlock her husband's computer. After some searching, she eventually found an encrypted folder she could decrypt using the same password. In it, she found several documents showing regular transfers from a Quantum Infotech bank account to several of her husband's numbered accounts. So far, the transfers

Future Dreams and Nightmares

totaled well over twenty million dollars. And she suspected that more were planned because two of the numbered accounts had yet to receive any funds. Once she used the same password to decrypt the thumb drive, she found it contained the same incriminating information proving her husband's embezzlement.

After printing out copies of the decrypted files, Alexis logged out of her husband's computer, carefully replaced the money, passports, notebook, and thumb drive in the wall safe, and returned the painting to its place on the wall. Then, after looking around the office for any sign of her having been there and finding none, she picked up the printouts and left.

I've got to get these to Jason, Alexis thought as she hurried to the garage. Now that she had learned what her husband had done, using Mr. Morgan's first name suddenly seemed natural to her. She took out her phone and called him. "Hello, Jason. It's me."

"Hello, Alexis," Jason said. "Are you okay? Did you find anything?"

"I'm fine. Jason. You were right. John's been embezzling from Quantum Infotech. I found the proof we need in the safe; he's been making huge transfers from his company to several overseas numbered accounts. The safe also contained a hundred thousand dollars in cash, three fake passports, and evidence he has a mistress. I'm on my..."

She had just reached the door to the garage when it unexpectedly opened to reveal her husband, John, and a younger woman she didn't recognize.

"Going somewhere, Alexis?" he asked. Then, grabbing the phone from her hand, he ended the call and dropped the phone into his pants pocket. Then he glanced down at the papers she was holding. "My, my, what have we here?" He took them, quickly skimmed each one, and frowned. "I can't have private company documents falling into the wrong hands, now, can I?"

Her husband turned to the woman next to him. "That was an excellent idea of yours, Emma, putting a trace on my computer to send us an automated security alert each time anyone logs in." He turned back to his wife. "Now, where are my manners? Alexis, this is Emma Meyer, Quantum Infotech's head of cybersecurity. Emma, this is my overly curious wife."

Alexis looked at the younger woman before turning back to her husband. "Why, John? You told me I was everything you ever wanted?"

"Alexis, your naivete and gullibility really are quite endearing. But your family's wealth and influence were always much more valuable to me, to anyone with ambition and the willingness to do what it takes to climb to the top. Now that I've found a kindred soul, you really aren't useful anymore."

Looking at the woman who had replaced her, Alexis finally noticed the pistol in Emma's hand. It was aimed at the center of her chest. She turned back to her husband. "What are you going to do now, John?" she asked. "You can't kill me again. No one is going to believe that I had another accident."

"Good question," he replied. "What do you think, Emma? We only need another five days to transfer the last of the funds to our accounts."

"We can't just keep her prisoner until then," Emma answered. "We don't have any safe place to keep her. Besides, if we let her go after we leave, what she knows could get us caught before we've had a chance to properly disappear." She paused for a second and then smiled. "No, I'm afraid your wife has been quite depressed these last few months, unable to handle the many evenings you've had to work late in the office. This time, she'll commit suicide. That way, everyone will think her boating and car accidents were earlier suicide attempts. By the time your staff at work notices the missing money, we'll have our new faces and identities."

John nodded. "You're right. But first, I need to shred these documents and check the safe to make sure everything's still there. Then I can guard her while you log in to my computer and check to see if she made copies of the files and emailed them to anyone."

"Okay, Alexis," Emma said. "You heard him. Move!" Once back in his home office, Emma pointed to a chair a few feet away from the wall safe and said, "Sit."

Alexis did as she was told. One question after another raced through her mind. Had Jason heard John's voice before the phone call ended? Was that why he hadn't called her back? Had he notified the police, and would they arrive in time to save her? She watched as her husband fed her copied documents into his paper shredder, destroying the physical evidence of his crimes. Would they think of checking her phone to find the photos she had taken? Would they learn she had been talking to an insurance fraud investigator? Had her phone call put Jason's life in danger?

Having finished shredding the documents, her husband walked over to the wall safe and opened it. He rapidly searched through its contents. "It looks like everything is still here," he said.

Meanwhile, Jason had arrived from the nearby restaurant. He recognized Mr. Huntington's candy-red gas-fueled Lamborghini visible through the mansion's open garage door. Entering the garage, he placed his hand on the car's hood. It was warm, confirming what Jason already knew from Alexis' interrupted phone call. Her husband had unexpectedly returned, and now she was in danger.

Jason drew his gun from its shoulder holster and walked over to the door from the garage into the rest of the mansion. He had feared that it would be locked, but it wasn't. Instead, the little light above the lock's keypad glowed green. Apparently, Alexis' husband had been in too much of a hurry to lock it. The house's alarm system wouldn't warn the man of his presence.

Jason opened the door and began his search for Alexis and her husband. Finding no one on the ground floor, he cautiously climbed the stairs leading to the bedrooms and Mr. Huntington's home office. Voices came from the office's open door. Besides Alexis and her husband, Jason was surprised to hear a woman's voice he didn't recognize.

Jason quietly crept up to the office door and took a quick peek into the room. Alexis was sitting in a chair in one corner of the room while Mr. Huntington stood several feet behind her with his back turned to the door. He was placing something into a wall safe while a woman with a gun stood next to Alexis.

Jason stepped into the room with his pistol aimed at the woman and shouted, "Freeze!"

The woman turned, raising her gun towards him. Both guns fired, and Jason felt a burning pain in his arm. The gun fell from his hand while the woman grabbed her chest, groaned, and fell backward.

Having seen the exchange of gunfire, Alexis reacted just a second faster than her husband and dove for Emma's gun. That gave her the time she needed to turn the gun on her husband as he lunged for her. Two more shots rang out. He fell on her, his entire weight knocking the wind from her lungs.

It took a second for Alexis to shove her husband's limp body off of her. She briefly aimed her gun at Emma as she scrambled to her feet, but quickly realized the woman was unconscious or dead. Then, with her husband and his mistress no longer threats, she turned to the man whose arrival had saved her.

"Oh my God, Jason! You've been shot!" Alexis said, looking with shock at the blood-soaked shirt sleeve.

"I noticed," he replied, trying to smile despite his clenched teeth. Blood flowed between the fingers of his hand tightly wrapped around his upper arm. "You'd better find something soon to stop the bleeding, or I'll be the one needing a resurrection."

Alexis nodded and rushed over to where her husband lay sprawled on the ground. His dead eyes stared up at her as she reached down and roughly yanked the tie from around his neck. Then, returning to Jason, she bound it tightly around his upper arm to staunch the bleeding.

"Who did I just shoot?" Jason asked as he stared at the woman bleeding on the floor. She moaned softly, struggling to breathe as blood filled her lungs.

"That's Emma Meyer," Alexis said once Jason's bleeding had slowed to a trickle. "She's Quantum Infotech's head of cybersecurity and my husband's mistress. They were just a few days away from finishing embezzling millions of dollars and disappearing with new identities."

"And what about you?" Jason asked.

"They were going to kill me and make my death look like a suicide!"

"Well, then, I don't feel so bad about killing her."

Alexis looked over at her husband's mistress. The woman's bleeding and labored breathing had stopped.

"House," Alexis said.

"Yes, Mrs. Huntington," the house answered.

"Call for help. There's been a shooting, and we need the police and an ambulance."

"Yes, Mrs. Huntington. Calling to report a shooting and requesting the police and an ambulance. Will there be anything else?"

"Let them in once they arrive."

"Yes, Mrs. Huntington."

Then Alexis sat down on the floor next to Jason while they waited for help to arrive. Neither spoke until they heard sirens sounding in the distance.

"You know, Alexis," Jason said, looking at her husband's body. "I don't think I can authorize payment for your husband's resurrection."

"That's okay, Jason," Alexis replied. "I won't be paying for it, either. For some people, one life is more than enough."

AUTHOR'S COMMENTS

Many stories have included increasing longevity by downloading one's mind into a clone when one is old or sick. But how would such an ability interact with the crime of murder when the victim can return from the dead?

ORIGINAL EQUIPMENT

It wasn't that Marcus Stone was against upgrades. Over the previous forty years, he had replaced his arms and legs with synthetic ones several times stronger than those he had been born with. His android torso contained a mechanical heart and highly efficient bioengineered lungs. His advanced digestive subsystem enabled him to stay healthy regardless of his diet. And his genetically engineered eyes provided excellent vision from the infrared through the ultraviolet and even included microscopic and telescopic capabilities. In every way, Stone's body was stronger, faster, more reliable, and more resilient. Equally important, the doctors could repair or replace parts as they wore out or newer technology became available, making him practically immortal.

And as Stone had risen through the ranks from a lowly worker to middle management, he had his brain augmented to remain competitive in the corporate rat race. With merely a thought, his internal router gave him mental control of his many devices, access the Global Cloud, and enter the many virtual realities the modern world offered. Moreover, the quantum hard drive at the base of his brain could store and retrieve far more data than the most powerful computer of only a few short

Original Equipment

decades earlier. And the embedded AI that was his personal assistant automated all his routine tasks so that he could concentrate on those few tasks that still needed a human's creative mind.

No, Stone was not against personal upgrades, far from it. His problem was their exorbitant costs. Even though the technologies were mature and widely available, the need for more competition between the small number of manufacturers kept the prices high. And so, he took out loan after loan to upgrade himself just so that he could remain competitive and pay off the balance of his prior loans.

But what else could he do? It was how the developed world worked, and so he continued, upgrade after upgrade.

...

When Dr. Evans entered the recovery room, Marcus Stone was still asleep. The doctor scanned the wall monitor beside the bed, checking Stone's vitals. The doctor ran a system diagnostic, and each of his patient's subsystems was operating within normal parameters. Dr. Evans smiled and then tapped a button on his tablet. "Time to wake up, Mr. Stone."

Stone opened his eyes, took a deep breath, and looked up at his doctor. "How did the procedure go?"

Future Dreams and Nightmares

"Exactly as planned," Dr. Evans replied. "I inserted the hardware upgrade and connected it to your other cerebral enhancements. Your new upgrade has increased your processing power by 43 percent, your memory by 500 terabytes, and your connection speed to the Global Cloud by two terabytes per second. So, when you return to work tomorrow, I'm sure you'll find your productivity equal or superior to the best of your coworkers."

"I should hope so," Stone said. "These constant upgrades are killing me. Each year, they get more expensive, and it will take me at least three years to pay off the loan I had to take out to get this one."

"I sympathize, Mr. Stone," the doctor said, "and I wish we could do something to lower the cost. But, unfortunately, Human Augmentation's virtual monopoly on cerebral enhancements leaves us no choice but to pass their costs on to our patients."

Stone sighed. "I understand." He got out of bed and stood up. "Are we done? You don't have any software uploads and installs to perform, do you?"

"No, we installed the latest software and drivers during the procedure. You're all set. It's extremely unlikely that you will have any problem with your upgrade, but if you do, just call the office, and we'll take care of it."

Stone turned to leave, but Dr. Evans stopped him. "Mr. Stone, I almost forgot." The doctor picked up a small glass jar from the table next to the bed. A blob of gray and white tissue, roughly the size and shape of a finger, floated in a clear liquid. "I thought you might like to see this."

Stone looked at it, not recognizing what he was seeing. "What's that, doctor?"

Dr. Evans raised the jar so Stone could get a closer look. "We needed to make room for your new hardware, so we had to remove the unnecessary cerebral tissue. This is the last of the original equipment you were born with."

AUTHOR'S COMMENTS

The source of this short story is the ancient Greek legend, The Ship of Theseus. According to Plutarch, Theseus rescued Athenian youths from King Minos's Minotaur and sailed with them to the island of Delos. Each year, to honor Apollo, the Athenians sailed the ship back to Delos. Over the centuries, every part of the ship was eventually replaced during its maintenance. The philosophical question is, "Is it still the same ship?" In this story, I ask the same question about a person who has all their organs and tissues replaced with upgrades.

A JUMP TOO FAR

I struggled to control my anger as I looked across the flag-draped coffin at each member of the team. They stood at attention in their black dress uniforms, the silver eagles on their collars polished and shining. Like them, I was also looking forward to avenging the death of our commander. Ortiz was stoic, her face emotionless. Her eyes stared back at me with the fierce determination she got when she had a disciple of Heaven's Host in her sights. Standing like a granite statue, Big Johnson's eyes were red and puffy as tears silently trickled down his cheeks. Manny, as short and wiry as Johnson was tall and beefy, looked as sad as I'd ever seen him. With his head bowed, Booker's lips moved in silent prayer. Finally, I looked at Beatrice, my beloved wife, comrade-in-arms, and steadfast friend since I joined the directorate. She gave me a barely perceptible nod, and I began.

"Commander Celeste Krieger was a born leader. Intelligent, tough, and tenacious, she was more than an outstanding officer. She was also a close and utterly loyal friend to each of us. We will all greatly miss her as we continue our work to achieve victory during the dangerous days and weeks ahead."

Recalling some of our missions together, I continued. "Commander Krieger was also damned lucky. Under her decisive leadership, we've had much more than our fair share of success. In the thirteen months since Heaven's Host killed Chancellor Roberts and all but one member of his cabinet, she helped us track down and eliminate 87 of their so-called disciples. We even killed and captured nine of those responsible for the assassinations, all while only losing three of our fellow agents."

I paused briefly, giving everyone a few moments to remember Sanchez, Avery, and Scott. We had lost them when a cell of disciples martyred themselves rather than allow us to take them captive. The three had just breached the disciples' hideout when their bomber set off the explosives that leveled the building.

"As your acting commander, I promise you this. We will continue as we did under Commander Krieger. The fanatical disciples of Heaven's Host claim their New Eden will be a utopian theocracy, but we know better. If we don't stop them, they'll replace our democratic republic with a religious dictatorship. If we don't stop them, New Eden will be a dystopian Hell on Earth. That is why we'll pursue these terrorists until every last one pays the ultimate price for their crimes. We will complete our mission of eliminating them, no matter how long it takes. And we will ensure that when we're at long last reunited with Commander Krieger for our final roll call, she'll smile as she welcomes us and say, 'Well done, agents. You did your duty, and you did me proud.'"

My AI silently vibrated three times in rapid succession, letting me know I had a priority message from Command. I touched my temple, where the tiny device lay just below the skin, and it silently spoke through my auditory implant. *Report immediately to the Director for new orders.* I subvocalized an acknowledgment and then returned my attention to my team. "That was the Director. It looks like we may have our next assignment. Get your equipment and be ready to deploy in 15 minutes. Dismissed."

Everyone saluted and headed for the door. I looked over at Beatrice, hoping for a reassuring smile as I went to get my first orders as acting commander. But she'd already turned away, her mind no doubt going over her predeployment checklist. She's all business when it comes to our work, and I didn't mind. Her professionalism was one of the first things that attracted me to her, and it made her one of the most effective members of our team. It has also kept us alive more than once.

Five minutes later, I exited the elevator on the top floor and entered the Directorate of Internal Security's Command Center. Director Donovan stood in front of the operations wall, studying a large map of the city. It showed dozens of green circles, each representing one of our agent's current location and status. About half were here in our headquarters building, while the others were scattered across the city in teams of five to ten. As I strode up to the director and reported for duty, I noticed that the eight circles representing one team in the industrial sector had yellow centers, showing their ongoing involvement in an active operation. As I watched, all eight changed from yellow to orange, indicating injuries. Then, four of the circles quickly changed to red, and two turned black. Two agents were dead, and six were wounded, four with life-threatening injuries. The words "Explosion detected" were displayed next to the team. One of the operations officers ordered two nearby teams to the location while another ordered an emergency medical evacuation.

Director Donovan shook her head. "In my office," she ordered, then turned and angrily limped to her corner office. I followed her in, ignoring the awe-inspiring view of the city below us through her floor-to-ceiling windows. Standing at attention, I waited for her to speak. Except for the scars that marred her face and hands, she looked much like her ubiquitous portraits that hung on the walls of most rooms in the building. She was the one council member who had survived the blast that killed Chancellor Roberts and the other members of his council. She touched the AI at her temple, subvocalized an order, and her eyes lost focus as she read the words scrolling across the inside of her contacts. Then, after what seemed like an eternity, but which couldn't have lasted longer than a couple of minutes, the tiny writing disappeared, and she stared into my eyes as if examining my very soul.

"Acting Commander Stevens, your record is exemplary with two letters of commendation and a Silver Star Second Class. It seems your late commander thought highly of you. She recorded her high confidence in your ability to lead. So, tell me, Stevens. Are you ready to advance from Acting Commander to Full Commander, with all the responsibilities and duties that entails?"

I only paused for a second before answering. "Yes, Director. I know I have big shoes to fill, but I'm also the most qualified member of my team." I knew it might have come across as bragging, but it was the simple truth. It may not have been how I envisioned my promotion, but I was confident I could lead what I considered one of the finest strike teams in the Directorate.

"Very good, Stevens. Now that you're a full commander, you need a briefing that is classified at the highest level. Report immediately to Section T, Sublevel 3. You'll have the official promotion in your records and authorization for the briefing by the time you arrive. You will excuse me for not accompanying you, but as you saw outside, I have a big mess in the Industrial Sector to clean up."

A Jump Too Far

A few minutes later, I was in an elevator heading down to Sublevel 3, where our research and development labs created the weapons and tools — both cyber and physical — we used against the enemies of The State. We all knew the labs existed down below, but none of our team except Commander Krieger had ever been there. And she had never told any of us what she saw, other than that it was critical to our eventual success, and we weren't cleared to hear about it. Like everyone else, I was curious, but we all knew better than to ask questions or speculate out loud.

The elevator slowed to a stop, and the doors opened to reveal two fully armed guards standing at port arms with their close-quarters automatics angled across their chests. I stepped out, and one escorted me down a wide corridor to a locked door labeled: Section T, Authorized Personnel Only. The guard stepped up to the door and stared into its security camera. It recognized him and announced his name and rank. The guard had me do the same, and the door said, "Commander Stevens, Marc. Access authorized." The door opened, and I walked in.

Dressed in the official uniform of the science directorate — a white lab coat, shirt, and pants — a tall man in his late sixties stood waiting for me. "Commander Stevens," he said, holding out his hand. His handshake was firmer than I expected, more like the grip of a field agent than a scientist, especially for a man of his age.

"I'm Dr. Evans, Director of Section T," he said. "I'll be giving you your commander's briefing. What I'm about to tell you is classified as top-secret and compartmented to a very select few with a need to know. No one outside of the Director, the Deputy Director, the people working in this lab, and agents with the rank of commander and above are authorized to hear what I'm about to tell you. That means no one on your team, not your wife, and certainly not your mistress, should you ever decide to have one. It also means not the disciples of Heaven's Host should they ever capture and torture you. Absolutely no one else. Do I make myself perfectly clear?"

I nodded.

"I need verbal confirmation for the record, Commander. Do you swear on your honor as a loyal officer of the Directorate of Internal Security that you will keep the secrets of Section T for as long as you live?" he asked, looking me in the eye. The tone of his voice made clear the critical nature of the information I was about to receive.

"I do," I answered. However, while I was certainly curious to hear the briefing, I also somewhat dreaded the associated responsibility. I didn't like the idea of not being able to share such important information with my team and especially my wife, whose counsel I greatly valued when dealing with difficult decisions.

"Okay, Commander. You will undoubtedly find what I am about to tell you strange. I know I still do, despite understanding the underlying physics and dealing with the technology daily." He unbuttoned the top of his shirt and used his thumb to hold up a metallic collar that circled his neck. A tiny green LED on it glowed softly, too dim to have been noticeable when hidden under his shirt. Then he reached into a pocket of his lab coat and pulled out another just like it. "As of this minute, Commander Stevens, this is your most important piece of equipment. More important than your AI. Even more important than your weapons," he said, handing it to me.

The collar consisted of two pieces, hinged on the back with two tiny prongs on one end and two corresponding holes in the other. I unbuttoned the top button of my shirt and put the device around my neck, sliding the prongs into the waiting holes. The collar clicked as its ends snapped together. Lightweight and flexible, it felt strangely warm against the skin of my neck.

"Very good, Commander," Dr. Evans said, smiling as I rebuttoned my shirt. "Your collar is going to be your constant companion from now on. You are not to take it off for any reason. In fact, you'll find that you can't take it off." I stifled the urge to reach up and see if what he said was true. "It will give you information critical for you to complete your missions. It will also act as a failsafe device. Should anyone — and I do mean anyone — attempt to remove it without the proper procedure and codes, the collar will self-destruct, preventing any adversary from discovering its secrets. Moreover, your collar — like your AI — will listen to every word you say, and the same self-destruct capability will thus also prevent you from revealing those same secrets."

While I didn't relish wearing an explosive ring around my neck, I knew I wasn't in the safest profession, and a disciple's bullet or bomb was far more likely to take me out.

"Follow me, Commander Stevens. I have something wondrous to show you."

Dr. Evans led me through a pair of security doors that formed a kind of airlock into a control room that looked out through thick panes of glass over a vast laboratory with high ceilings. In the center stood a metallic globe, some fifteen feet across, inside three concentric rings that slowly circled it, each rotating around a different axis. Dozens of small cables connected the strange device to the control room, while several massive ones connected it to what appeared to be major electrical power supplies. Ice-covered hoses connecting large liquid nitrogen canisters to the device's base gave off clouds of dense fog that slowly drifted across the floor. I had absolutely no idea what I was looking at and even less of what it could possibly have to do with helping me lead my team. I wondered whether it might be some entirely new kind of computer to predict the whereabouts of the disciples and their next targets, but I was totally guessing.

"That, Commander Stevens, is TOTS, our Timeline Observation and Travel System," Dr. Evans said with evident pride. "We use it to observe hundreds of nearby timelines almost identical to our own. Then, by looking at what the disciples of Heaven's Host do in these different versions of our universe, we can statistically predict what they will do on our own timeline. But more importantly, we've recently discovered how to use TOTS to actually jump to timelines that give us the best chance of eliminating them."

"I don't understand," I said, trying and failing to wrap my head around what I was hearing. "What the hell's a timeline, and what do you mean by jumping to another version of our universe? And what's the point of going to a different universe to fight their Heaven's Host when our enemy is in this universe?"

"Follow me, Commander, and I'll attempt to explain." Dr. Evans led me into his office, closed the door behind us, and walked up to a blank wall.

"Commander, believe me, I know it is a lot to take in. Maybe it will help if I draw a picture as I explain." Dr. Evans turned and used his finger to draw a long straight horizontal line on the wall. He labeled the left end with the word *past*, a dot in the middle with the word *now*, and the right end with the word *future*. "A timeline is merely a way to represent the dimension of time, running in a line from the past through the present and into the future. We travel along our timeline, moving at a constant speed of one second per second from our past into our future. All clear so far?"

"I guess so," I said, wondering why he bothered to state something that sounded so obvious.

"Okay," Dr. Evans continued, drawing several more lines parallel to the first one. "According to quantum physics, there are an infinite number of timelines all parallel to each other, like an infinitely large bundle of fiberoptic cables. Each timeline represents one way that time could unfold, based on the infinite number of random choices that elementary particles can make. For example, on one timeline, an atom emits a photon of light in one direction, while on a neighboring timeline, the same atom sends the photon in a different direction. The infinity of these infinitesimal choices adds up to one version of how the universe can unfold. It's like the multiverse theory, except only our universe is real. The other universes are merely *potentially* real."

A Jump Too Far

Dr. Evans paused for a second to see if I was still with him, then continued. "Now, it's important to understand that all these nearby timelines are quite similar to ours." He stopped and drew a stick figure next to the dot labeled *now* on our timeline. "Currently, we are on this timeline, which represents the universe as it was, is, and will be. But TOTS enables us to view and even jump to other nearby potential timelines. When we jump to another timeline, it becomes real, and our old timeline becomes merely potentially real." He touched the stick figure on the original timeline and dragged it to a nearby timeline, producing a dashed line connecting the timelines. "So, if all the timelines are interchangeable, and we can jump to another, then why not choose to jump to a timeline that helps us win our war against Heaven's Host? We can be on any nearby timeline, so why not be on one in which we win, and they lose?"

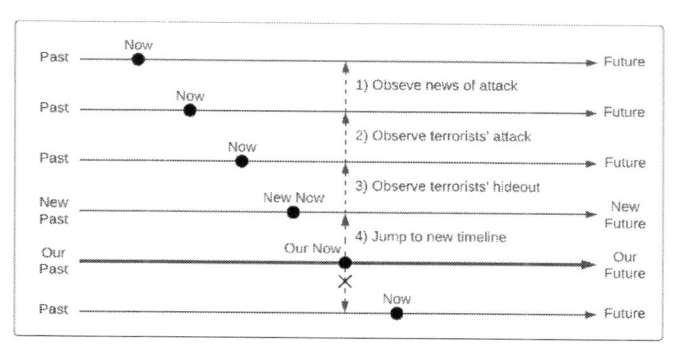

Past	Now		Future
Past	Now	1) Observe news of attack	Future
Past	Now	2) Observe terrorists' attack	Future
New Past	New Now	3) Observe terrorists' hideout	New Future
Our Past	Our Now	4) Jump to new timeline	Our Future
Past	X Now		Future

I thought I was following him, but something about his description didn't seem quite right; I just couldn't put my finger on it. The look on my face clearly told him he hadn't convinced me yet.

"Commander Stevens," Dr. Evans said, "you really don't have to worry about this. We have everything under control. To continue, it is important to understand that quantum randomness means that the *nows* on different timelines are not perfectly synchronized. On some timelines, our *now* corresponds to minutes, hours, or days in their future. On other timelines, our *now* corresponds to their past. We take advantage of these differences and use TOTS to observe the future of nearby timelines and discover what the disciples of Heaven's Host are doing. Once we understand their plans, we will tell you exactly where they are and what to expect. Then we select an optimal timeline for us and jump to it."

Dr. Evans pointed at his neck. "This is where our TOTS collars come in. Those of us wearing them will know when we've jumped because they will quietly vibrate when we change timelines. We will be the only ones who remember the events of our previous timeline. For everyone else, it will be as though nothing has happened. After the jump, we typically notice a few trivial changes, especially chaotic things like the weather. For instance, it might instantly change from sunny to cloudy, or we might notice inconsequential changes in the products being advertised, such as alternative names or new packaging. But the only thing that matters once you feel your collar vibrate is that you will now have the intelligence you need to be in the position to take our fight to Heaven's Host."

I smiled. Good actionable intel is like gold to a miser because an operation's success depends on knowing more than the enemy. I finally understood Commander Krieger's previously inexplicable good luck that had made our team so successful and kept most of us alive. How she knew what kinds of weapons the disciples would have and where they were hiding. She'd kept us from walking into more than one ambush, and now I knew how. Still, something gnawed at me. "But Dr. Evans," I argued, "I don't see how using your machine helps us find the disciples, no matter how many other timelines you observe. With their safe houses and sympathizers helping them, we have a very tough time finding them with all our Directorate's other resources. It sounds like instead of looking for a few needles in our huge haystack, you're just giving us more haystacks to search through. Surely, it's got to be harder finding them in the other timelines' haystacks."

"Well, Commander," Dr. Evans said, "there is a significant difference between the disciples of Heaven's Host and your needles in a haystack. Unlike needles, the disciples are terrorists and only feel successful to the degree to which they cause enough widespread terror to force us to permit them to set up their Second Eden. Thus, their strong preference for explosives and very high-profile assassinations. It's relatively easy for us to use TOTS to spot such high-visibility events."

"Okay, I think I'm getting a basic handle on the timelines and *nows*, but I still don't see how you get all the information I need to disrupt their operations and take them out."

"Here's how we get you what you need," Dr. Evans said. "First, we identify and observe a timeline in which our *now* is in their future, the disciples have struck, and the news reports their terrorist act. Now we know what they are going to do, including when and where. Then, we find and observe a timeline in which our *now* is less far in their future so we can observe the attack, identify the attackers, and see when and how they arrive. Then, by observing a series of timelines in which each of their *nows* is just a little bit nearer to our own, we can trace the disciples back to their hideout and even farther back in time so that we know how long they are going to be there. This enables us to know when and where we can best attack them. Finally, it is just a simple matter of jumping to a timeline that gives us adequate time to prepare ourselves and stop the attack before it begins. It's really quite ingenious, though it takes a great deal of effort to explore several hundred nearby timelines, determine their temporal offsets from ours, and gain the data we need to jump to the specific timelines we want."

"But I was just upstairs in the command center when one of our teams in the Industrial Sector was ambushed. There was an explosion, and we lost two agents. The rest were injured, some of them critically. How'd that happen if TOTS lets you know what will occur?"

"As far as discovering that attack," Dr. Evans answered, "TOTS is neither omniscient nor omnipotent, and we are scientists, not gods. Our technology allows us to make highly valuable observations and excellent predictions based on these observations. But we can't observe everything, and we can't predict every contingency. We also can't always jump to *exactly* the timeline we choose. There is inescapable quantum randomness due to Heisenberg's Uncertainty Principle, which limits what we can do. We can greatly improve your chances, but we can't guarantee your success. And there is always human error, and that applies to field agents as well as us scientists and engineers. I'm not sure what happened in this case. I wasn't aware of the attack until now. But I can assure you we will discover what went wrong and work to see that it does not happen again."

Future Dreams and Nightmares

"But can't we just jump to a timeline where the attack hasn't happened yet and avoid the ambush?"

"Unfortunately, we can't jump to timelines where our *now* is in their past," Dr. Evans explained. "The limitation of only being able to jump forward in time prevents us from changing *actual* events that have already happened. That could lead to all manner of temporal paradoxes, which the laws of the universe prevent. So, Commander, there's sadly no way now for us to jump to a timeline that would enable us to undo this recent attack on our agents. Once someone is dead, they're dead, and we can't bring them back."

I nodded, disappointed and frustrated that there was no way to go back in time to save Commander Krieger.

"So, do you have any further questions before I finish this briefing?

I only had one more. "What about our counterparts in the new timeline? When we jump, won't that mean there will be two of each of us?"

"Not at all, Commander Stevens. Because we jump to *potential* timelines, the people on them aren't real but merely potential. When we jump, they become us, or we become them, if that's how you prefer to look at it. Just remember that only those of us wearing our special collars will remember our past from previous timelines. Everyone else will only remember the past they experienced on the new timeline. For them, it will be as if nothing has changed."

There was a knock on the door, and an operator came in. "We've completed our surveillance, Director. We have a solution and are ready to jump."

"Excellent," Dr. Evans replied. "Make the jump." We left his office and walked up to the large window overlooking the laboratory and TOTS's big metal ball. A warning buzzer sounded, and red lights began flashing in the next room. The concentric rings sped up, spinning faster and faster until they became a blur around the globe.

"All clear," an operator said before flipping up a safety cap covering a large red button. "Jumping in three, two, one, and zero." He pushed the button. The ball flashed a brilliant blue light that left a large spot before my eyes, and I felt a faint vibration from my collar. Otherwise, I couldn't tell that anything had changed.

Dr. Evans gestured around the room. "You see, Commander Stevens, we're on a new timeline, and everything is the same as before the jump. Except, of course, the clock on the wall has jumped seven minutes into what used to be our future, and more importantly, we now know where to send you." His eyes briefly lost focus as he glanced through the data scrolling across his contacts. Then he paused to subvocalize an order to his AI.

Instantly, the same information scrolled in front of my eyes. Six disciples were in an old, abandoned house in Wilmington Heights, a rundown sector overrun with meth labs, crack houses, and climate refugees, most of whom hadn't worked in months, if not years.

"Okay, Commander," Dr. Evans said. "We've done our part. Now, it's up to you and your team. Six disciples have just entered one of their safe houses, and our computer predicts they will remain there for another hour and forty-eight minutes. That means their bomb-maker has probably not finished with the bombs they'll use to blow up several transmission towers bringing electricity into the city. Given the neighborhood where their safe house is located, I would leave as soon as possible and take them out before they leave. Happy hunting." And with that, he turned and headed back to his office.

I had my AI notify my team that we had a bomber and five of his buddies to take out ASAP. I headed for our armory to suit up, and once properly armed and armored, I took the elevator to the garage and my waiting team.

...

I was sitting shotgun in the lead SUV as our caravan made its way through deserted streets. The sun had set over an hour ago, and a cold November wind blew hard out of the Northwest. I silently went over

A Jump Too Far

our plan of attack for the fourth or fifth time, looking at the video stream from our drone circling high overhead. As black as our SUV, it was our invisible eyes in the night sky. I switched from night vision to ultra-wideband radar, and the roof of the building became transparent. As TOTS predicted, the six disciples were still inside. Two stood guard by the front door, one stood by the back door, two sat on a couch in what looked like the living room, and one worked at a table in the kitchen. That would be our bomber.

Five minutes out, I switched back to night vision and watched as our four SUVs spread out, each taking a different route so that my team and the three other teams converged on our objective from all sides. Manny, who was driving, pulled into a narrow alley, killed the headlights, and slowly inched forward until I could see the disciples' safe house about a block down the street. I smiled, thinking there was no way they could know it was no longer safe. We climbed out and got our heavy weapons while Ortiz unloaded several small robots onto the ground. One by one, I glanced at my team, and each nodded, indicating their readiness. In their identical black body armor and with their helmets' visors down, they were practically invisible in the darkness. To avoid the need for nametags that could permit potential adversaries to identify us (and thus our families), our helmet-mounted displays showed our names floating above our heads like the halos of avenging angels. But, of course, standing half a foot over everyone else, I didn't need my HMD to tell me which one was Big Johnson.

The other three teams reported in. Once everyone was ready, I put our plan into action. I told my AI to send in our ears, and it passed on my orders to our little robots. They rolled off to place microphones on the outside walls of the house. In less than a minute, everyone on our four teams could hear the disciples talking and moving about. Two were arguing over the relative merits of their favorite football teams. We also heard footsteps and a door opening and then closing. I switched back to radar imaging and saw that one of the two guards at the front door was now sitting on the toilet in the bathroom. He was going to be pissed when he realized he'd left his rifle leaning against the wall near the other guard.

"Okay, everyone," I said. "You all know your assignments. Let's get this done. I'm going to be really pissed off at anyone who lets the bomber blow us up tonight, so take him down before he even thinks of setting anything off. And remember, I want at least two of the bastards alive for questioning."

Gang graffiti covered the house's boarded-up windows, and someone had replaced the original doors with steel ones that would require a little extra persuasion to open. We set large charges on the doors, smaller ones on the windows, and a little one to cut the electricity. Four of our agents were in place to launch tear gas and flash bangs through the windows the instant the charges blew. We backed off a few paces, and as soon as everyone reported ready, my AI simultaneously set off the explosives. The combined blasts were deafening, even through our helmets with their built-in noise filter. The flash bangs went off a second later, and I knew no one in the house could hear or see anything for the next minute or two. Meanwhile, I watched the operation unfold via the UAV's radar feed. Our teams poured in through the now empty doorways, dropped the bomber and the two guards holding their weapons at the front and back doors, and had the remaining three tased and unconscious before I counted to five.

I walked in and looked over the place. The guy in the bathroom didn't even have time to get up and seemed rather pathetic, sitting on the toilet with his pants around his ankles. Big Johnson was none too gentle as he picked up the limp man, yanked his pants up, buckled his belt, and hoisted him onto his shoulders like he was carrying a dead deer back to his pickup. I hoped toilet man had time to finish his business. Otherwise, the agents in the minivan pulling up outside to take custody of our prisoners would bitch about the smell all the way back to the Directorate.

Although my helmet display showed everyone in the green, I followed protocol and had each member report their status. One by one, they sounded off. No one mentioned a problem, and I thought my first operation as the commander had been textbook perfect until I heard Big J growl. "Should have waited another couple of minutes, Commander. The damn asshole wasn't finished and went and shit himself when I threw him over my shoulder. Apparently, he had the runs 'cause now it's running down my armor."

"Thanks for the sitrep," I answered. "Ride back with the extraction team. I'm sure they'll enjoy the personal air of distinction you've brought to an operation. It practically reeks with the sweet smell of success."

Big Johnson groaned as he turned and carried off his prisoner. When the forensics and clean-up teams arrived, everyone walked back to their respective SUVs. Once inside our vehicle, we raised our visors. I looked in the back, and everyone was smiling and looking smug.

Beatrice, who sat behind me, leaned forward and gave me a quick kiss. "Good job, honey," she whispered. "It doesn't get any more by the book than this."

I smiled, looking forward to getting home and spending some quality alone time with her once we put Tim to bed and the nanny had left for the night.

Then I noticed a lock of her hair sticking out from under her helmet. It was distinctly auburn instead of brown. Maybe it was because of the funeral, getting my promotion, or the briefing, but I hadn't noticed she'd dyed her hair. It was a nice color that went well with her hazel eyes, and I was surprised I hadn't picked up on it until then. Whether it was a new dress or lipstick, I knew she hated it when I failed to notice. "By the way, I really like your hair like that," I whispered as she pulled back.

She gave me a slightly confused look, and I wondered if she thought I was teasing her for having helmet hair. "Like what?" she asked as she pushed the loose hair back under her helmet.

"The color," I replied. "It looks good on you. Not sure why you haven't tried it before."

Now I could tell she was really confused, even a bit concerned. "Are you all right, Marc?" she asked. "You didn't get hit on the head by something when the charges went off, did you?"

"No," I answered, wondering why she reacted so weirdly to my compliment.

"My hair's been this color for over a year."

Now it was my turn to be confused. Then I remembered Dr. Evans warning me about how jumping to a new timeline could cause insignificant changes. I guessed this must be one of them. "Never mind, beautiful. Probably just a trick of the light." I realized I would have to be more careful about what I said after a jump. Otherwise, she'd know I was keeping secrets from her, which was never good. No, never good at all.

...

The following two months flew by with little free time to consider the ramifications of what I'd learned in Section T. We made four jumps, resulting in four highly successful operations with only three injuries, none of which were serious. I also learned just how much of a commander's time was taken up with administrative duties like reading the agents' operational review reports, writing my summary reports to be sent up the management chain, leading training and proficiency maintenance exercises, and holding performance reviews. While a part of me understood the need for my new managerial responsibilities, I now understood why Commander Krieger used to call such work "administrivia." I began to long for the days when I rarely had to deal with the paperwork and when Beatrice and I could leave work together instead of me coming home one, two, or even three hours after she and our son had already had dinner.

Though she tried to be understanding and didn't blame me for spending less time with her and especially with Tim, I could tell my increased workload had been getting to her. She became moody. But when I tried to talk to her about it, she

A Jump Too Far

just told me not to worry and that we both knew things would change once they promoted me to commander. She said we'd just have to find a way to adapt.

Ignoring the problem wouldn't help, so I decided to do something about it. That coming Sunday was our fifth wedding anniversary, and I bought tickets to one of her favorite musicals, a romantic comedy playing at the Rialto. I also made reservations at a fancy restaurant she's been talking about trying. It was in the West Hills overlooking downtown, and I reserved a table with a view. Finally, I bought the necklace she'd been dropping hints about. Yep, I had the situation covered.

...

We were at our training facilities thirty miles south of town, practicing taking down disciples in an abandoned factory or warehouse. Because there are so many places the bad guys could hide to ambush us, it is critical that everyone maintains top proficiency. Unlike individual houses or apartments, where speed and explosives can overwhelm a small number of adversaries before they know what hit them, big buildings are different. Such operations called for stealth, finesse, and the ability to clear each room in an organized manner, so we didn't overlook anyone who might outflank us.

Future Dreams and Nightmares

Then it happened. My collar vibrated, followed a few seconds later by my AI letting me know I needed to contact Command. "Okay, everyone," I told my team through the headphones in their helmets, "Practice is over. Gather your gear and meet me back in the parking lot. Looks like we've got some real work to do."

My AI relayed the details of the operation to me. Three months ago, disciples of Heaven's Host had stolen radioactive material from a company that produced medical devices that irradiated tumors with gamma rays. They used the stolen material to make a dirty bomb they intended to set off in the middle of downtown.

Captain Peters would command our attack. Twenty-three disciples were meeting in a large farmhouse surrounded by empty fields. The captain wisely decided that a direct assault on the house was too risky because of the lack of cover. Instead, he decided that we'd wait until the meeting ended. It would be a large operation involving five teams. Three squads, including the one I'd lead, would ambush the convoy of five cars carrying eighteen disciples on the road once they left the farm. Another team would attack the five disciples remaining in the house, while the fifth team would guard the farm's perimeter to make sure none of them escaped into the surrounding countryside.

A Jump Too Far

Some twenty minutes later, video from our drone revealed the terrorists' five-car caravan leaving the farmhouse. We had set up our ambush in a wooded area half a mile down the road we knew they would take. We had felled a small tree and planned to attack their convoy when they stopped to clear the roadway. But the disciples didn't fall for our trap. Instead of pulling right up to the fallen tree, their lead car stopped at least fifty yards back from it. We waited a few minutes, thinking they were merely discussing what to do before pulling the rest of the way forward.

But we were wrong. Apparently, our recent series of successful operations had made the terrorists highly suspicious and careful. Their convoy's two rear cars started turning around, apparently intending to take another route into town. Simultaneously, two men got out of the lead car, opened its trunk, and pulled out shoulder-fired rocket-propelled grenade launchers.

I yelled, "Incoming!" as I dove to the ground.

The men fired their grenades toward our hiding spots on either side of the road. A second later, the grenades exploded, pelting us with shrapnel and shards of broken trees. I jumped back up just in time to see one of them firing a third grenade, this time at the fallen tree blocking the road. The resulting explosion split the tree in two and blew its halves apart just far enough for the disciples' three remaining cars to drive through.

"Here they come!" I yelled as the two terrorists jumped back in their car. "Don't let any of the bastards get past us!"

Our uninjured agents staggered to their feet, and we placed half a dozen rounds into the lead car as its passengers used assault rifles to rake our positions with lead as the car raced by. We had more luck with the following vehicles. At least one lucky shot hit the second car's driver, causing it to clip the fallen tree and flip onto its side. The third car plowed into the rear of the second car, igniting its gas tank and engulfing both vehicles in flames. I ordered everyone to cease firing, but by then, we had riddled both cars with over a hundred bullet holes. Between the fire and our bullets, no one was left to take into custody for interrogation.

The sensors in our body armor did not detect any radioactivity, so the dirty bomb and the rest of the radioactive material had to be in the lead car or the two cars that turned around. That meant the city was still in danger. I ordered one team to chase after the lead car and another team to pursue the two cars that had turned around while my team and I would tend to our fallen. In total, we had three agents dead, including Booker, and two injured, one with a gunshot to the shoulder and the other with shrapnel wounds from a grenade. I called in our losses, and we secured the scene while we waited for our injured to be picked up for transport to a hospital.

All in all, our mission so far had been a complete shitshow, and all I could do was hope that the other teams and any that the Directorate held in reserve would stop the terrorists. Otherwise, the Heavenly Host would get the terror they so desperately wanted.

Within a quarter hour, two medical helicopters arrived and landed, with their main rotor blades barely fitting between the trees on either side of the road. Medics rushed out and began working on our two injured agents. They quickly loaded the agents and took off for the closest hospital with a trauma center. Meanwhile, we waited for an extraction team to arrive and pick up the bodies of the dead.

Beatrice found me standing over Booker's body and the bodies of the other two dead agents. Deep in thought and self-recrimination, I tried to think of what I could have done differently to have kept them alive. I didn't notice her until she took my hand.

"There was nothing you could have done differently," she said as she stepped in front of me. "Our plan to ambush them was sound. It should have worked. There was no way you could have known they'd stop so far back and fire grenades at us."

"I got complacent," I said, shaking my head in disgust. "We've been so successful these last few months, I should have realized the disciples would be paranoid. This mission was too important to them for them not to be. I could have had a couple of snipers nearer to where they stopped. If I had, they could have taken out the disciples with the grenade launchers before they fired at us. If I had, Booker would still be alive."

"You can't know that," she replied. "Our job is deadly dangerous, but worth the risk. Booker knew that. We all do. Booker is dead because of the damned disciples, not you."

She was right, but I still felt guilty. We stood there in silence, keeping vigil over our dead. Then my collar vibrated. Suddenly, Beatrice was no longer holding my hand. Instead, she was leaning against me, with her head on my shoulder and her arm around my waist. We had jumped to a new timeline.

Fifteen minutes later, the extraction team arrived to take over the site from us. I called the remaining members of my team. We climbed into our SUV and headed back to the Directorate.

We were almost there when our AIs notified us of an incoming announcement from the Director. "Today, I have the sad duty to inform you we have lost seven of our comrades-in-arms. The terrorists also injured another twelve agents, three of them critically. But I want you to know that their sacrifices were not in vain. We prevented Heaven's Host's most audacious attack since their assassination of Chancellor Robert and all but one member of his cabinet. Today, we saved lives and prevented the terrorists from exploding a dirty bomb in the city center that would have spread radioactive dust throughout the downtown area. Although our citizens may never learn of the heroism of our fallen, we will never forget."

I looked around the SUV at the members of my team. Although still grim-faced over Booker's death, I could also see their fierce pride and hunger for revenge. They assumed our success was due solely to the efforts of our brave field agents, but the vibration of my collar and Beatrice's simultaneous change of position told me that TOTS and the operators of Section T shared the credit. Too bad my team could never know just how much our successes depended on their work.

...

Two days after Booker's funeral, the evening of our wedding anniversary arrived. I took a very surprised Beatrice out to eat at the fancy restaurant on the high hill overlooking the city.

"I hear the food here is excellent," I said once a server had shown us to our table. The view of the city laid out below us was spectacular.

She picked up the menu, scanned the prices, and frowned. "It should be, given these prices. Did you get a raise you forgot to tell me about?"

"No," I said. "I just wanted to take you out someplace special to celebrate." Then, taking out the box containing the necklace she had told me she liked, I said, "Happy Anniversary, Beatrice."

"Marc, our anniversary isn't until next month."

"What?" I asked. I knew today was our anniversary. My AI always reminded me of important dates, so I wouldn't forget them.

"Marc, today is July 17th, and our wedding isn't until August 17th." Her voice had the hard edge she used when she was angry with me. "And you agreed we couldn't afford this necklace. I told you I didn't want it now that we know Tim needs two more surgeries to fix his shattered leg. You keep forgetting little things, and you even got the date of our wedding anniversary wrong. And now, you're spending money we don't have on a fancy dinner and a necklace we can't afford. You've been acting strangely ever since you got your promotion."

I couldn't hide the shock on my face. *Tim has a shattered leg? But he was fine this morning!* Then, I realized that was before the jump. I was in this new timeline, and I couldn't ask Beatrice what was wrong with our son without her thinking there really was something seriously wrong with me. "I'm sorry, Honey. I forgot," I lied, once more hating that

A Jump Too Far

I couldn't tell her about TOTS and the timelines. Still, Dr. Evans had said that the differences between timelines were insignificant, but Tim being injured and requiring more surgeries was hardly a minor change.

The more I thought about it, the more I realized each time we'd jumped to a new timeline, things had gotten progressively different. I needed to talk with Dr. Evans. Maybe the probability of a significant change increased the farther we jumped from our initial timeline.

"No, I'm serious, Marc. Something's going on with you, and it has me worried. What aren't you telling me?"

"Beatrice. Nothing's going on. It's just the stress of the job and the extra hours." At least that lie was half true. God, I wished I could tell her the whole truth. "I'll take back the necklace tomorrow and get our money back."

She looked at me, and I could tell she didn't believe me. The secrets I had sworn to protect stood like an invisible wall between us, and we ate most of the rest of our meal in silence. I was glad when we went home early because I was worried about Tim and desperately wanted to know how he was and how he got injured.

Once we arrived home, I immediately went to Tim's bedroom while Beatrice sent the babysitter home. He was still awake and watching TV. His

Future Dreams and Nightmares

entire right leg was in a cast with several rods sticking out of it, apparently holding the bones together until they knit back together. "How are you doing?" I asked, pulling up a chair and sitting down next to him.

He turned to me with an expression that was both a smile and a grimace of pain. "It hurts, and I can't find a comfortable position."

"I know, son. I wish there was something I could do to make it magically heal faster, but some things just take time."

We watched the rest of his movie together, and I stayed with him until he eventually fell asleep.

Meanwhile, Beatrice had gone to bed, and the lights were off when I entered our bedroom. I crawled in beside her, but she had her back turned to me. I wasn't sure if she was asleep, but regardless, I felt like there was an invisible wall between us. Unable to stop thinking and worrying about how TOTS and jumping timelines were ruining my life, it was several hours before I eventually fell asleep.

The following morning, I went down to Section T to talk to Dr. Evans. I told him about my son and how secrecy was affecting my marriage.

He tried to be sympathetic but quickly turned our conversation into a lesson on time travel and reality. "Commander Stevens, you forget we used

TOTS to make dozens of jumps before we issued you your collar. You believe that your memories of your wife and son before then accurately reflect what actually happened. But you're wrong. They don't reflect how events occurred in humanity's original timeline. Your memories of your life before you put on your collar aren't any more real than your wife's memories in the current timeline before the jump. Both were merely potential memories of potential events until jumping made them real. Reality is relative to our current timeline. Change timelines, and you change reality. Despite our memories from the previous timelines, they are now false memories. I know it can be very difficult sometimes, but you must learn to accept the reality of this timeline." He paused. "That is, until our next jump."

...

A few weeks later, I was briefing the Director on the results of my team's yearly performance reviews when a TOTS analyst interrupted us.

"Excuse me, Director, Commander," the analyst said. "We've identified a new Heaven's Host attack, this time on the Gaithersburg fusion reactor complex. A successful attack will interrupt electricity to the Capitol and most of eastern Maryland and Virginia, potentially for several weeks."

"Have you traced the terrorists back to their base yet?" Director Donovan asked.

"We have," the analyst replied. "They're currently hiding in a warehouse in North Potomac."

"How many are there, and how long do we have before they leave?" I asked.

"At least a dozen disciples of the Heaven's Host, Commander," the analyst answered. "We can't be sure how many remained there after the others left to attack the power plant. And you'd better hurry if you intend to hit them at the warehouse." The analyst glanced at the wall clock in the Director's office. "We only have one hour and 17 minutes before they leave for their target. I'll send the details and video of their operation to your AIs."

"Okay, make the jump," the Director ordered.

"Yes, Director," the analyst replied before turning and jogging back to the TOTS control room.

The Director turned to me and said, "Commander Stevens, I'm placing you in overall command of this mission. Take Charlie and Echo teams with you and use three of the helicopters. You'll never get there in time if you drive."

"Okay, Director," I said. "We'll leave as soon as the teams are ready." As I headed back to our team's arming room, I had my AI notify my team of our mission. I also ordered them to jock up and

A Jump Too Far

meet me at the helicopters for immediate transport to the warehouse where the terrorists were preparing for their attack.

In less than ten minutes, I had put on my body armor, grabbed my assault rifle, sidearm, and spare magazines, and taken the elevator up to the helipads on the roof. The three helicopters already had their rotors spinning, and the last few agents were loading their equipment. I climbed aboard my team's helicopter and glanced around the cramped cabin. Because we were all wearing our helmets with our protective visors lowered, my AI displayed everyone's names above their heads. Since the helicopter held the expected number of agents, I didn't bother reading the names that floated like textual haloes over their heads.

I had my AI set up an encrypted channel with the three teams. "Okay, everyone. You've all been sent the information we have on the terrorists and the warehouse where they're preparing their attack." I checked the time on my helmet display. "The terrorists intend to leave in about 35 minutes, so we're going to hit them while all the snakes are trapped in the same hole. Here's how we are going to handle this. Team Charlie, I want you to take the back of the warehouse. My team will take the front. Team Echo, you can take the sides. The helicopters will surveil the perimeter and take out any of the bastards that manage to escape. You all know what to do. You've got five minutes to get into position. We hit them in six."

My AI displayed a timer that steadily ticked down from six minutes. Our helicopter immediately began lowering us into the parking lot in front of the warehouse while the other two pulled away to deliver their teams to their designated locations. If we had had more time, I would have preferred to arrive less conspicuously. The terrorists undoubtedly had lookouts, who were no doubt warning the others of our arrival. Imagining the frantic activity inside, I hoped their haste would cause them to make mistakes that would make up for our loss of surprise.

Besides a standard entry door leading to a front office, the front of the warehouse included three garage doors that were big enough for large trucks.

"Ortiz and I will take the front door. The rest of you will breach the far garage door. We go in when the timer reaches zero."

The others prepared to blow the garage door while Ortiz and I took up positions on either side of the front door. Then, assuming the door was locked, Ortiz placed a much smaller charge on its deadbolt.

The timer reached zero, and Manny's explosives blasted a large hole in the garage door. Ortiz and I gave the terrorists guarding the front door a second to be distracted by the explosion. Then Ortiz blew the deadbolt, and we rushed inside. Several bullets pinged off my armor as we made quick work out of the three men guarding the door. Having cleared the room, we moved into the central open area of the warehouse, where the sound of small arms fire seemed to come from every direction.

We probably hadn't taken more than a half-dozen steps before the bomber martyred himself and the other Disciples of the Heaven's Host by setting off the explosives they had intended to use against the power plant. The blast knocked me off my feet and slammed me into a nearby wall.

By the time I came to, the engagement was over. All the terrorists were dead, either killed by us or by the explosion. My head pounded from when it struck the wall, making it difficult to think. I had my AI display the statuses of the three teams under my command. We had lost two agents from Charley team, one from Echo, and Ortiz from my team. Including my concussion, we had seven agents injured, two critically. Big Johnson and Manny were okay, but I couldn't find Beatrice on my display. She wasn't listed as dead or injured. She was just gone. And my AI listed an agent Michel Steinbrenner as a member of my team. *Who the hell is Steinbrenner?*

Manny was leaning over me. "Are you okay, Commander?"

"How's Beatrice?" I asked. "There must be some glitch in my AI. She's not listed on my display."

"Who's Beatrice?" he asked.

What? "What do you mean, 'Who's Beatrice?'"

"I'm sorry, Commander. I have no idea who you mean."

"Sergeant Beatrice Stevens," I said.

He shook his head.

"The fifth member of our team. Beatrice, my wife."

"Commander, you must have really hit your head. I think you must have a concussion. I've never heard of a Sergeant Beatrice Stevens, and you're the only Stevens on our team."

On the drive back to Directorate HQ, I used my AI to find out who agent Michel Steinbrenner was. According to his records, he had been a member of my team for over a year. Even more disturbing, human resources had no record of the Directorate having ever employed a Beatrice Stevens, and my employee file listed me as unmarried!

Growing increasingly scared and upset, I had my AI widen its search parameters, and it found several women with the correct first name and birthdate. A few seconds later, it came back with a list of seven potential matches. Scrolling through them, I discovered my wife was a police detective.

A Jump Too Far

Worse, she had married someone she dated in college, and they had two children.

I went ballistic. On arriving back at the Directorate, I stormed up to the Director's office and barged in.

"That last jump cost me both my wife and child!" I yelled.

"What?" Director Donovan asked, looking up from some documents on her desk.

"You heard me. On this timeline, Beatrice isn't a member of my team. She's never been an agent, and we didn't meet at the academy. Hell, we've never even met, and our son was never born! And now, I find out she's a cop who's married to someone else, and they even have two kids!"

"That's terrible news, Marc," she said sympathetically, as she stood up and walked over to me. "I'm very sorry to hear that. I want you to feel free to take some time off to process your loss."

"Time off?" I exclaimed incredulously. "I don't want any damned time off. I want my family back!"

"Marc, I'm afraid that isn't possible. And I must warn you not to contact your previous wife. You've got to remember that in this timeline, she has no idea who you are. You can't tell her or anyone else about TOTS, and besides, she'd never believe you. To her, you'd just be a dangerous mentally ill stalker with a crazy delusion."

"Damn it, Director. That's not good enough. You've got to jump us back to a timeline where I still have my wife and son!"

"I'm afraid I can't do that, Marc. We can't use TOTS for personal reasons. We can only use it for official Directorate business like combatting terrorists."

"God damn it! You're the Director. You decide what's Directorate business. You can order the operators to take us back."

"I'm sorry, Marc, but I won't. And I can't. Besides, what makes you think you're the only one suffering because of a jump? At least Beatrice is alive. I had a husband and two children in the original timeline. But our ninth jump took us to a timeline in which my husband died in a car wreck a year before we were to have met. Yet as devastating as losing my husband and children was, that jump enabled us to prevent the disciples of Heaven's Host from poisoning the city's water supply. Losing my husband and children was the extreme price I paid to save hundreds, maybe even thousands, of innocent lives."

She sighed, and her shoulders slumped as she relived the pain of her loss. "That's why we can't permit our personal desires to outweigh our duty to The State. You and I have sworn an unbreakable oath to end this terror campaign by the disciples of Heaven's Host. We cannot fail in our mission of stopping these neofascist evangelical zealots from creating their Second Eden and replacing our democracy with their theocratic dictatorship. We have no choice but to do our best and have faith that in the end, our best will be enough."

...

With no way to undo the jump and with my wife and son lost to me, I had no choice but to carry on as best I could. Each of the following eight jumps resulted in successful missions, and I gradually came to terms with my personal loss.

Then, the unthinkable happened. Immediately after the next jump, my TOTS collar vanished. One second, it was vibrating, and the next instant, it was gone. I immediately had my AI place a high-priority call to the Director. But her AI responded she was currently occupied and would return my call as soon as she was free. Next, I tried to contact Dr. Evans, the head of Section T, but he was also busy and would get back to me later. I tried to concentrate on leading our current mission and ignore the unexplained loss of my collar, but I grew increasingly worried as several hours passed without a response from either of them.

It was only later, as we were returning to the Directorate, that I received the following message from the Director, which she had broadcast to everyone with a TOTS collar.

"Immediately after our last jump, every TOTS collar disappeared. It has taken us until now to discover what happened. In the current timeline, the physicist, Dr. Masters, died in a car crash several years before he discovered the temporal theory underlying parallel timelines and the technology enabling us to jump between them. Therefore, TOTS does not exist in this timeline, and it disappeared at the same time as our collars. There is no secret Section T in the basement of the Directorate headquarters building, and Dr. Evans and his staff of engineers and operators are now scattered across the country in different corporations and academic institutions, trying to understand the lives they've been dropped into without warning. It will take many months, and potentially several years, to acquire sufficient funding to reinvent and replace what we have lost. In the meantime, we have no choice but to continue our fight against Heaven's Host without the advantages TOTS has given us. Our work will be more difficult and dangerous, but I know you will do your duty as you always have, with honor and professionalism. And with God's help, we shall prevail."

AUTHOR'S COMMENTS

In this time travel short story, I wanted to address jumping between timelines rather than merely moving back and forth on the same timeline. I also wanted to show the potential negative unexpected effects that jumping between timelines might have on people doing the jumping.

WE SERVICE ALL

As usual, Jack had nothing to do except remain alert in case something went wrong. But nothing ever did. The autopilot fired his trusty old cargo ship's massive engines in the exact direction for precisely the correct duration. The ship skipped several times on the deep atmosphere's upper edge before slowly sinking like a giant steel stone into a world-sized pond. Initially high-pitched, the sound of the thickening air rushing past his ship's stubby wings grew louder until it drowned out even the roar of the engines. After being weightless for fifteen months, the sudden return of weight was both reassuring and yet strangely disconcerting. The critical time of reentry passed, and the ship made several slow turns to cut its speed before making its final approach to the spaceport. Then, the ship smoothly touched down and rolled to a stop in front of the customs hanger.

As always, Jack's cargo of luxury items and alien artwork should bring a hefty profit. Hopefully, it would make up for the loneliness of spending so many empty days, weeks, and months by himself in the silence of his ship. But it never was.

Sometimes he wondered why he spent so much time with only his old cargo ship as a companion. But, remembering his wife's accident and untimely death, he knew the answer. He knew no one could ever replace her. And alone in space, no one ever would.

Though the credits in his account grew and grew, no matter how wealthy he became, they would never be enough. His wife was gone, and a perverse part of him wanted to suffer. He should have been with her, died with her, but he hadn't. And so, he lived the monastic life of a penitent in an era without monks and monasteries, just him alone in his silent crypt of a ship.

Still, no spacer could stay in space forever. Jack had to land, deliver his cargo, refuel his vessel, and take on new cargo and supplies for his next run. And to do that meant landing at a spaceport, a place where those who would service the spacer, as well as his ship, would eagerly cater to every imaginable need and desire. And every time Jack landed, he would do what every spacer did. He would indulge his senses and seek contact, even if only for a few hours, in exchange for some meaningless credits that otherwise lay unused in his account.

Jack opened the hatch and stepped out onto another new world. Never had he been so far from Earth. The warm afternoon air was heavy with strange scents, as if smoldering sticks of exotic incense surrounded his ship. Several low hills stood beyond the short blocky buildings of the nearby city. Their vast forests of purple plants produced an oily haze that merged smoothly into the low-hanging clouds.

"Excuse me, sir," a voice said in perfect English. "Welcome to Mårtõðħt."

Jack looked down to see two of the planet's inhabitants waiting for him at the bottom of the ramp. Standing only a meter and a half high, each had four stubby legs and four long arms jutting at right angles from its roughly spherical body. Thick strands of what looked like greenish spaghetti covered the pair, starting just below what he took to be a circular mouth surrounded by eight small yellow eyes. The pair appeared identical, their only difference being the number and color of the small pouches that hung from the harnesses they wore.

One held a translator above its mouth and spoke in a soft series of clicks and unpronounceable consonants. "Excuse me, sir," the device translated. "Welcome to Mårtõðħt. I am the port customs inspector, and my colleague is from the Finance Guild. We are here to assess your import duties and landing fees. We have the manifest you transmitted and are now ready to inspect your cargo."

Jack looked at the pair and was glad that their translator understood English. He knew he couldn't even come close to pronouncing the local language. "Certainly," he replied. "How long before I can begin unloading?" The translator emitted another series of clicks and consonants.

We Service All

"We should finish by midday tomorrow," the customs inspector answered. "Perhaps until then, you would care to visit our city. I am sure we have many fine restaurants that can prepare food suitable for your taste and nutritional needs. And you will surely enjoy staying in one of our fine hotels after so many nights confined aboard your ship."

"Thank you," Jack replied. "I look forward to it."

"Please authenticate your identity here, and you may go," the translator requested as the customs inspector handed Jack a tablet and pointed one two-fingered hand at a glowing circle on its screen. "We shall communicate with you tomorrow once we complete your inspection."

Jack touched the circle, and the tablet took and recorded a microscopic sample of his DNA. Once the tablet confirmed his identity and registered him, it made a brief ticking sound, and the circle ceased glowing. Jack handed the tablet back and left the spaceport in search of a good meal and some of the human contact he had avoided for so long.

Just outside the terminal building, Jack saw the typical establishments found in any port city. First came dozens of restaurants. Each competed for the attention of newly arrived spacers with brightly colored signs, sound clips praising the talents of their cooks, and hidden fans blowing tempting smells out onto the sidewalk. Catering to offworlders unable to read their menus, their wide windows held enticing samples of local foods and recreations of the most popular dishes from neighboring star systems. Although most meals merely lay on their plates, Jack noticed that several menu items had holographs of writhing worms and chittering insectoids.

After walking a few blocks, Jack began to see the same dishes over and over. Finally, having no way to evaluate their quality, he entered a restaurant at random. Once inside, he led a server out to the front window and pointed at what he hoped would be a reasonably safe selection. The server noted Jack's choice and then led him back inside. Jack selected a table that was roughly the right height and sat down in a reasonably appropriate chair, even though it was backless and nearly three times as wide as he needed. Before long, the server trotted up to him and set down a plate, the contents of which looked remarkably like the sample he had seen in the window. The server paused as Jack took a bite. To Jack's surprise, he found that the meal tasted quite good, though it was dry, and its texture took some getting used to.

"I need something to drink," Jack said, pantomiming raising a glass to his mouth.

"Måmkt dog ðħ," the server said, looking at Jack with two of its yellow eyes.

"I don't understand you," Jack answered. "Are you asking me what I want to drink?"

"Måmkt dog ðħ," the server repeated, raising two of its hands up and over the mouth at the top of its rounded body.

Jack nodded his head. When that brought no response, Jack pointed to a cup sitting on a neighboring table where three locals appeared to be engaged in a lively conversation.

"Måmkt dog ðħ ðåmwk," the server replied and left.

Again, having no idea what the server had said, Jack turned back to his food. He was almost done when the server returned with a large glass of boiling water. As usual, dining on a new planet was an adventure, and if ordering boiling water to drink was the only problem, he would count his dinner as a success. After paying by pressing his finger to the glowing circle on the server's tablet, Jack got up and went out into the night, looking for a place to satisfy his second hunger.

Jack did not have to search long. Leaving the main road and walking farther from the spaceport, he soon found the district he was looking for. The flashing signs became brighter and more garish. Eschewing recorded come-ons, each establishment had a barker standing by the front door, working hard to entice potential customers inside. And the samples in the windows were now holographs, showing members of various alien races.

Jack assumed the holographs were of beautiful females, at least beautiful in the eyes of others of their species. But Jack knew he was more often wrong than right. One could never assume anything when dealing with exobiology. Alien planets were not populated by mammals, and many were not even vertebrates with spinal columns. Intellectually, he knew he was more closely related to cabbages than all creatures that had evolved on other worlds. And sex for different species often meant anything from hermaphroditic couplings to species with three or more sexes. Some parasitic species even needed hosts for mating.

Still, to each his own, Jack had learned to say. Prejudice was bad for business and something a successful trader could ill afford. He moved farther into the district, looking for just a single brothel with a human woman. Though the larger establishments serviced the needs of many species, he could not find even one with a hologram of a woman in the window.

Beginning to believe that he was too far from home, Jack was just about to head back and look for a hotel when he noticed a side street lined with several smaller establishments. Not holding out much hope, Jack nonetheless decided that he might as well see what they offered before giving up. The brothels were shabbier, and their selections were considerably fewer than the larger establishments. He was turning to leave when a Deltinoid came up behind him.

"Both farrr frrrom home, Earrrthling, you and I," the creature said. "Perrrhaps I can be of serrrvice."

Jack turned and looked suspiciously at the being he took to be the brothel's barker. The Deltinoid looked like a huge twelve-legged purple caterpillar if you ignored the two trunks at its head and the fact that circular scales covered its body. Jack glanced back at the window to make sure, but he only saw two holographs, and they both showed members of the indigenous species. "I don't think so," Jack replied, feeling tired and frustrated by his lack of luck. The thought of spending the evening ogling a naked Deltinoid dancer did absolutely nothing for him. In fact, the idea was more than a little revolting, especially were he to think the encounter through to its obvious conclusion. Over the years, he had heard the occasional rumor. Some sick spacers would get so lonely they eventually succumbed to interspecies sex. Although some spacers felt pity for the sick bastards, Jack thought the idea was disgusting and couldn't imagine ever getting that desperate.

"Hasty conclusions often false, Earrrthling," the Deltinoid said as Jack turned to leave. "Ignorrre window. My establishment now can serrrvice all. You thirrrsty. Come inside. Have drrrink. You see. We serrrvice all."

The barker was either perceptive or had somehow guessed how little of the hot water Jack had drunk at the restaurant. Finally, realizing just how thirsty he was, Jack decided at least to go in for a quick drink. Just one drink and then back outside to search for a hotel.

Inside, the place looked like any small brothel on a dozen systems. There was a bar, a few small tables for the drinking customers, a well-lit runway for the local lovelies to dance on, and the unmarked door in the back that led upstairs to the privacy chambers. Jack sat down at one of the tables, ordered an overpriced drink containing more alcohol than water, and glanced over at the evening's entertainment.

On the stage in front of a Danubian spacer was another of his species, rippling and rocking rhythmically to the sounds of cymbals, gongs, and tubular bells. She was tall, slender, and looked vaguely like the product of the mating of an insect and a porcupine. She snapped her claws like castanets while the color of her carapace alternated between green and purple. Jack had to admit that she seemed to be working hard to convince the Danubian to go upstairs with her. But seven empty

We Service All

bottles littered the spacer's table, four of his six eyes were closed, and he was close to comatose.

The music eventually stopped, and the prostitute's dance ended. She looked over at Jack and started moving towards him, her claws clicking softly on the stage. Becoming increasingly ill at ease, Jack was considering moving to a table farther back when the Deltinoid returned with his drink.

"No worrry, Earrrthling," the creature said as he placed the glass containing a bright blue liquid on the table. "Drrrink. You see. We serrrvice all."

Jack took a long, hard gulp and felt the spicy liquid burn his tongue and throat as he looked back up at the stage. The Danubian dancer stood over him, close enough to reach down and touch him with her long spidery forelimbs. A slow seductive song from Earth began to play, and she started to sway to the music. Jack chugged the rest of his drink, and the fiery taste brought tears to his eyes.

Something was happening to the Danubian dancer, something Jack couldn't explain by the drink or the tears that blurred his sight. The dancer seemed to melt. Her claws were retracting, sliding back into her forelimbs. Then the spines along her back withdrew into her body. In less than a minute, she had morphed into a smooth gray mass that still swayed rhythmically with the music. The transformation continued. New arms grew outwards as the gelatinous torso raised itself onto two new legs. Hands appeared and grew fingers, while a head formed, sprouting ears, eyes, and a nose. The gray skin turned a light beige as breasts blossomed and a groove formed where its legs met its body. Completing her transformation, her bald head sprouted shoulder-length blond hair while a small patch of identically blond hair hid the groove below. In less than two minutes, the Danubian had transformed into the most stunningly beautiful naked human woman Jack had ever seen or even dreamed of in the depths of his solitude between the stars.

"You see, Earrrthling," the Deltinoid said. "No lie. You have seen with yourrr own eyes. We serrrvice all."

Jack was dumbfounded. The woman before him swayed gracefully to the music, her right arm held modestly before her ample breasts while her left hand hid the treasure between her legs. He looked at her as though she were some magician's assistant, suddenly appearing from the box that briefly before had held a snarling tiger.

The music became Chinese, and the dancer's hair turned from blond to black. She looked at him with brown almond eyes, and her large breasts were now smaller, though no less enticing. The buxom Swede had become a demure East Asian beauty. Then the music moved westward, and she transformed into a Bollywood dancer, followed by

We Service All

an Arab belly dancer, then African, and finally back to Caucasian, though this time a redheaded Irish Coleen.

"But how?" Jack gasped. He didn't dare look away lest the magician might perform another switch if he glanced at the barker for even the briefest of moments.

"Amazing, isn't she? A Bluuuvoxian shape-shifterrr. Only one on entirrre planet, and I have herrr. I pay herrr well, but she morrre than worrrth it."

The beautiful dancer took his hand and gently pulled him to his feet. Then, without realizing it, Jack placed his thumb on the proprietor's tablet and transferred the necessary credits. He followed her through the unmarked door and up the stairs to one of the waiting privacy chambers.

"I can be any kind of woman you desire," she said with only the faintest of accents. Her hair and skin changed color. She grew taller, then shorter. She went from thin to muscular to Rubenesquely soft and sensuous. She even took on the faces of several famous actresses and singers from previous centuries. "I can be anyone," she whispered as she unbuttoned his shirt and then kneeled to remove his pants. Then, standing once more, she moved forward until her naked breasts lightly touched his chest with each breath.

Her skin was wonderfully warm and smooth as he took her in his arms and kissed her. Her lips were soft, her perfume intoxicating.

"I can do anything you desire," she breathed as she reached down to take him in her hands. "I can fulfill your every fantasy, satisfy your every need."

His desire grew, and he could feel his body respond to her gentle touch with an overwhelming lust he hadn't felt in years. But suddenly, the memory of her as he had first seen her returned unbidden to his mind. He remembered the Danubian dancer with a spiky carapace, razor-sharp teeth, and claws instead of hands. His manhood wilted, and his lust vanished as though it had never existed.

She drew back as if physically struck by the intensity of his loathing, both for her and for himself. "But that is not me," she cried. "Look at me!" she begged, gesturing at her perfect body. "This is me. This is what you want and need."

But it wasn't. Jack's memory teleported him back to his former home on Earth, to the tragic accident that had taken his wife some twenty years earlier. Trembling, he sat on the bed, reached down, and picked up his tablet from where it had fallen. Tapping its surface, he brought up a holographic image of his wife. He didn't want a prostitute, even one who could become the most beautiful of women. He wanted only one woman, the one woman he could never have again. He wanted his wife. But she was dead and buried long ago on a planet hundreds of light-years away.

The prostitute sat down on the bed, gently turning his hand so that she could look at the image he could barely see through his tears.

"I understand," she said, placing an arm around him and gently pulling him to her breast. The simple act was no longer sexual but comforting as her face morphed into that of his long-dead wife. A skilled empath, she gingerly searched through his memories. She found the sound of his wife's voice, her mannerisms, her way of speaking, and, most importantly, his memories of their most tender and intimate moments together. Expertly, she used her telekinetic talent to carefully manipulate the neurotransmitters in various areas of his brain. She delicately lowered his norepinephrine level, easing his stress. She gently elevated his serotonin, dopamine, and oxytocin levels to increase his feelings of well-being and deepen his feelings of love.

"Jack," she whispered. "Look at me, Jack."

He slowly looked up, and there she was, looking exactly as she had on their wedding night. "Sarah?" he asked, confused.

"Yes, Jack," she whispered, increasing his trust by further elevating his oxytocin levels.

"But..."

"Hush now, my love," she said. "Everything is finally as it should be." She gently eased him back on the bed, holding him in her arms and gently stroking the back of his neck. "Hold me in your arms and tell me you love me. Tell me all the things you've waited oh so many years to say. Tonight, I am yours."

And so, they held each other. They talked for hours, and when they finally made love, it was truly an act of love, far more emotional than physical. And afterward, as they lay together and he fell asleep, she ever so slowly and carefully retook her natural form. Her body softened, losing its human form. Then, beginning at his feet and gradually moving up his legs and torso, she gently flowed around him until she had surrounded him, enveloping him in a living blanket that returned him to the dark, warm safety of the womb.

And while her patient rested in a dreamless sleep, the Bluuuvoxian healer used her innate telekinetic abilities and decades of psychological and psychiatric study at her planet's famed medical monastery to heal Jack's broken mind. She strengthened certain memories, weakened others, and repaired the holes that depression and loss had torn in his soul. And when she had finally finished her work, she gently withdrew from his mind and body. Then, retaking the form of his wife, she leaned over, kissed him softly one last time, and tenderly tucked the covers around him.

Then the Bluuuvoxian healer quietly left the privacy chamber and headed back downstairs to wait for her next patient. The long, lonely voyages between systems tended to attract spacers with psychological problems, and their weeks alone in the void only worsened their troubles. Nevertheless, she had found that working in brothels near spaceports was an efficient way to find the broken ones and fulfill her sacred vows to heal damaged minds. She was naturally interested in learning her next patient's identity and species, but it was only a matter of professional curiosity rather than preference. As a Bluuuvoxian healer, she serviced all.

AUTHOR'S COMMENTS

One of science fiction's powers is it enables authors to view cultural norms and taboos from an alien's perspective.

CLOSE ENCOUNTERS OF THE FOURTH KIND

The Honorable Arthur Henderson, Earth's Minister of Alien Affairs, was working on the new Arconian trade and cultural exchange treaty. Its details — including the Arconian's demands for expanded access to several of Earth's colonies — had been giving the minister migraines for weeks. That is why Henderson was more than happy to put the treaty aside when the recorded message from Jonathon Jeffries, Earth's ambassador to the Borgal Alliance, popped up on his screen.

Henderson clicked on the message's icon, and the ambassador's video began to play. "Hello, Arthur. I just received a copy of an interesting report from a Borgal exploration ship that I think you'll find interesting. About two months ago, they discovered and mapped an apparently uninhabited water world on the far edge of Borgal space. The ship's sensors didn't detect any of the usual signs of intelligent life from orbit. There were no radio communications, electricity generation and consumption, cities, large-scale aqua- or agriculture, or land and water transportation systems. Thus, the world seemed ripe for Borgal colonization. Apparently, the ship's captain was on the verge of claiming the planet when a low-flying shuttlecraft spotted a village of hunter-gatherers in a jungle clearing."

That's unexpected, Henderson thought. First contact almost always involved species that had at least mastered such essential electromagnetic technologies as electricity and telecommunications.

"The Borgal sent down a small first-contact team that produced the preliminary report I just finished reading. It covers only the most basic information about the inhabitants' biology, culture, and language.

"Per the Stellar Alliance's Unaligned Alien Protection Treaty, the Borgal placed the world on the official list of protected planets and notified the ambassadors from the other alliance members and me of their discovery. And since the Borgal couldn't colonize the newly discovered world, and it didn't seem to offer them any possibility of significant trade, the exploration ship merely transmitted its report back to Borgal and continued on."

That makes sense, Henderson thought. Like the East Indian Company of the 18th and 19th century Earth, competing Borgal trading companies controlled access to Borgal space. If a Borgal company couldn't trade with or exploit a planet for financial gain, the planet would be unworthy of its interest.

Future Dreams and Nightmares

"When I was reading through the Borgal report," the recording continued, "two things really piqued my interest. First, the inhabitants (who identified themselves as the kex) are roughly humanoid, which suggests a potential for easier communication with us. Second, as far as the Borgal biologist could tell, the kex have only a single sex that gives birth to live young. The biologist, therefore, labeled them as a female-only species."

Humanoid, Henderson thought. *Not exactly a common body type. And it would be nice to have a species in the Stellar Alliance that might be easier for us to understand.*

"Arthur, I recommend you read the Borgal report attached to this message. I also recommend that we send a first-contact team to Kex. Because the Borgals restrict alien spacecraft from traveling through their space, our team will need to park their ship inside the hold of a larger Borgal vessel for the rest of the voyage to the Kex system. However, a Borgal trade route passes relatively close to the Kex system, and I can arrange passage for our team both to and from the planet. Let me know what you decide. End message."

While not a high diplomatic priority, Minister Henderson agreed with his Borgal ambassador that sending a small first-contact team to learn more about the kex would be worthwhile. To limit the risk of an accidental, gender-related faux pas, he decided an all-female team would be best. He had his personal AI assistant create lists of relevant available personnel and made his selections.

Minister Henderson chose Deputy Ambassador Kathleen Helms to lead the first contact team and act as the interim Kex ambassador. At 36 years old, Helms was relatively young to lead a first contact mission, but she had recently returned to Earth after doing excellent work supporting Ambassador Jeffries. In addition, her being fluent in both spoken and written Borgal would undoubtedly prove useful when dealing with the crew of the Borgal trader.

The 32-year-old Dr. Kalisha Jackson was Minster Henderson choice as the team's exoethnologist to study the kex's culture. After receiving her doctorate in alien anthropology from Tuskegee University, she had spent a dozen years studying the Linga on Tau Ceti F. Until then, the Linga's early industrial age society had the most primitive technology of any species with which Earth had made contact.

Because an expert linguist would be essential to the mission's success, the minister picked Dr. Long Li. As the oldest member of the team, the 68-year-old professor of alien languages would be their interpreter, document the Kex language, teach the other team members to speak Kex, and program translators for them to use until the others had mastered the language.

Next, he chose Dr. Samantha Resnick as the team's exobiologist and medical doctor. The 39-year-old biologist would study kex biology and the biology of the planet's flora and fauna.

Henderson also selected Colleen Thompson (28) to pilot the team's ship and Jill Stevens (31) to be the engineer responsible for maintaining the ship and the team's equipment.

Finally, his choice to complete the team was the 26-year-old Captain Jessica Walker to ensure the team's safety, hopefully in a manner that avoided conflict with the native population.

...

Three months and two jumps later, the Earth Spaceship Magellan reached the border of Borgal space. Although it was not a small vessel, measuring some 25 meters wide and 60 meters long, the Magellan was dwarfed by the much larger Borgal trading vessel Fisk, which would take the team the rest of the voyage to Kex.

The Fisk followed a regular route connecting seven Borgal colonies, repeating the same series of jumps every 207 days. Ambassador Jeffries had arranged for the Fisk to make an additional stop in the Kex system, where the team would take the Magellan down to the surface. The Borgal trading vessel would then pick them up the next time it passed by.

As the team's linguist, Dr. Long had the most work to do during the trip to Kex. She spent the majority of the voyage in her cabin studying the recordings the Borgal explorers made during their meetings with the indigenous villagers. By the time the Fisk arrived in orbit above Kex, Dr. Long had the tentative beginnings of an English-Borgal dictionary. She could also speak along with the kex in the recordings, even if she didn't yet know the meanings of many of the words. Although the human vocal tract could never exactly mimic the Kex spoken by the natives, Dr. Long still spent many hours working to minimize her human accent. Finally, she had taught the others the most important words that she was confident she had correctly translated.

...

After stopping at three Borgal colonies, the Fisk finally entered the Kex system, and the day of Earth's first contact with the kex arrived. The team gathered on the bridge of the Magellan and strapped themselves in for the short flight down to the planet's surface.

Ambassador Helms looked at each member of her team and said, "I know you're all professionals, and you know this, but I'm going to say it, anyway. We must all remember that our primary mission is to establish *friendly* relations with the kex. That means we have to earn their trust and convince them to view us as friends. Our secondary mission is to learn everything we can about them, their culture, and their planet. To be successful, we need to not do or say anything they might consider insulting or threatening. And we need to avoid making any social faux pas. That means we need to be polite. And when we screw up (and we *will* occasionally screw up), we need to immediately apologize and convince them that any violation of their customs or taboos was unintentional and caused by our ignorance.

"The kex will undoubtedly have some customs that we might find objectionable, unethical, or illegal in terms of Earth law. We might find some of their customs to be personally immoral or even disgusting. But we must always remember that this is their world, and it is not our place to pass judgment on them. As the saying goes, 'When in Rome, do as the Romans do.'

"And finally, Captain Walker, I fully understand you are responsible for ensuring our safety. Nevertheless, any use of force against the kex must be an absolute last resort. And even then, the force must be proportional and the minimum amount needed to prevent a team member's severe injury or death.

"Are we all clear on this?"

The rest of the team agreed by nodding or saying some variation of "Yes, Ambassador."

"Okay, then. Colleen, let's get this mission started."

Colleen Thompson, the ship's pilot, brought the Magellan's nuclear reactor up to operating temperature and notified the Borgal ship they were ready to depart. The colossal trading vessel's landing bay doors opened to reveal the planet spread out below them. With its hundreds of small islands scattered beneath salmon-colored clouds, the water world sparkled in the light of its orange dwarf star.

Ambassador Helms looked over Thompson's shoulder as the pilot studied the feeds from their ship's sensor arrays. "So, what do you think, Colleen? How accurate was the Borgal report?"

"It was spot on," Thompson replied. "Kex is a pretty extreme example of a water planet with 97 percent of its surface covered by a single worldwide ocean. The only land consists of several chains of volcanic islands, surrounded by reefs enclosing shallow lagoons. The largest islands are roughly the size of megacities, but the vast majority are tiny and uninhabited."

"What about signs of civilization?" Dr. Jackson, the exoethnologist, asked.

"I'm not picking up any radio or microwave transmissions," Thompson replied, "so it doesn't look like they've developed any forms of telecommunication. I'm also not seeing signs of industry, aviation, or shipping. There are no major or even medium-sized cities, and most of the mid-sized islands only have a few simple villages supported by fishing and small amounts of farming. It basically looks like Polynesia before contact with European explorers."

Ambassador Helms nodded. "Land us on the island where the shuttle from the Borgal trading vessel made first contact. That way, the kex will be less shocked to see aliens. Since it was on a small island with only a single village, we can also learn more about the natives and their culture before we move on to their largest town on the biggest island."

"Will do, Ambassador," Thompson said as she slowly eased the Magellan out into space. Once safely away from the larger Borgal vessel, she fired the ship's main engines, and the super-heated hydrogen exhaust decreased their orbital speed. A few minutes later, Kex's gravitation lowered the Magellan into the planet's atmosphere, where friction burned off all but a tiny fraction of the rest of its forward momentum.

An oval island appeared on the horizon. Its central volcano towered above rolling hills covered in a thick rainforest of purple vegetation. A narrow, forested plain led down to broad beaches of black sand and a light blue lagoon bordered by a ring of coral reef.

"There's the village," Thompson said, pointing to a clearing containing a large wooden structure surrounded by a couple of dozen smaller huts.

"It looks like the natives are using the nearby clearings for farming," Dr. Jackson, the exoethnologist, observed. "We won't make a good impression if we land on their crops."

"I'll set her down on the beach," Thompson replied.

"Bring us down a couple of kilometers from their village," Dr. Jackson suggested. "That way, we'll be close enough to be convenient while hopefully being far enough away that they won't view us as a threat."

Several minutes later, the ship settled gently onto the beach with its bow aimed at the nearby tree line and stern just a few meters from the water's edge. Microphones mounted on the hull picked up the soft sounds of small waves lapping on the shore, the buzzing of bugs, and the squawks of colorful flying creatures the ship's landing had disturbed. Then, a deep booming of a drum came from the direction of the village.

"Apparently, we got the villagers' attention," Dr. Jackson said.

"What do you think?" Ambassador Helms asked the exoethnologist. "Should we go to them or wait for them to come to us?"

"Let's let them make the first move," Dr. Jackson replied. "This is their island, and no one likes a pushy guest, especially someone who shows up uninvited."

A few minutes later, Captain Walker pointed towards the forest's edge, some 25 meters from the bridge's forward windows. "We have company."

Several kexes were standing just inside the tree line, staring at the spaceship with large, wide-set eyes.

Slowly, one of them stepped forward onto the beach. The size of a twelve-year-old girl, her arms and legs ended in large, webbed hands and feet, and her long flat tail nearly reached the ground. The tiny, silvery scales that covered her naked body sparkled in the red light of the midday sun. Stopping ten meters back from the ship's bow, she spread her arms and held her four-fingered hands open.

"Is she welcoming us?" Ambassador Helms asked.

"Perhaps," Dr. Jackson replied. "Or perhaps she's merely showing us she's unarmed and comes in peace."

"Either way, it looks like it's time to make first contact," Ambassador Helms said. "Li, let's go see how good your Kex is. Jill and Colleen, I want you to stay on board and guard the ship."

Descending the gangway onto the beach, the exotic smell of the alien forest and sea was powerful after so many days of breathing the Magellan's filtered and recycled air. Despite the small size and relative coolness of Kex's orange dwarf star, the air was warm and humid because of the planet's proximity to its sun. They stopped five paces from the kex, who waited patiently for them to approach.

"Greetings," the alien said, speaking in her native language. "I am Vax. As the village eldest, I speak for my people. I welcome you to our island."

Dr. Long stepped forward and replied in Kex. "We thank you, Eldest. My name is Dr. Long Li. My companions and I come from planet Earth."

"Earth?" Vax asked.

"It is a world that orbits a star on the far side of Borgal space."

"When night comes, will you show me this star?"

"Unfortunately, it is too far to see without a telescope, a device that makes far-away things appear much closer than they really are." Dr. Long gestured to the others. "As I am the only one who has studied your language, my colleagues will carry small translation devices until they also learn your language. You can speak to them, and they will understand you. Their devices will also let them speak to you in your language."

"That is indeed a most marvelous skill," Vax said. "It seems there are many things you can teach us."

Dr. Long introduced the other members of the team. "This is Ambassador Kathleen Helms. She is our Eldest and speaks for Earth, our planet. And this is Dr. Kalisha Jackson, who is trained in the study of alien cultures. This is Dr. Samantha Resnick, who studies alien biology and is our healer. Finally, this is Captain Jessica Walker, who is responsible for our safety. Colleen Thompson, our pilot, and Jill Stevens, our engineer, remain onboard our ship."

The Eldest nodded to each of the others as Dr. Long introduced them. "When the Borgal traders foretold the coming of outworlders having bodies like our own, my people and I were curious. But I must admit, I am surprised by your lack of a tail, the smallness of your hands and feet, and their lack of webbing. Surely, such disabilities must severely limit your swimming. Can I, therefore, assume that there are no oceans on your world?"

Dr. Jackson replied, whispering so the kex could better hear her device's translation. "Eldest, seas cover some 70% of our planet Earth. We humans, however, are creatures of the land. We have, therefore, not evolved adaptations such as yours for swimming. Perhaps you can teach us your ways of the sea while we teach you our ways of the land. Thus, both of our species may gain knowledge and a better understanding of each other."

"That is wise," the Eldest observed. "As we say, 'Do not ask a fish to climb the mountain.' It is not the fish's fault it has no legs."

Ambassador Helms spoke next. "As Dr. Long said, we have traveled a very great distance to meet you. We humans hope to learn about your people and your planet. In exchange, we will happily teach you about our world. We hope that our arrival will be the start of a long, peaceful, and beneficial relationship between our two species. We, therefore, request your permission to park our ship on this beach so we can easily visit your village."

"Your request is granted," the Eldest replied. "You may freely visit our village from sunrise to sunset, but please remain away during the night unless I send for you or grant you permission. We will likewise avoid your beach after nightfall."

"Thank you, Eldest Vax," Ambassador Helms replied. "As the sun is now overhead, perhaps you would like to escort us to your village? We would very much like to see it, and I suspect your people are curious to see us."

"Of course," Vax replied. "Follow me, and I will lead you there."

The entire village had turned out and was waiting for them when they arrived.

"Look at the adults' abdomens," Dr. Resnick said. "Almost all of them are in various stages of pregnancy. I can't think of another species with such a high pregnancy rate. I wonder how they've avoided overrunning the island."

"They must have a high mortality level," Dr. Jackson said. "Maybe they have a high miscarriage rate or many deadly childhood diseases. Before the development of vaccines and antibiotics, many human infants and young children died from preventable diseases. Or maybe it's the adult death rate that's high. Fishing beyond the reef could be especially dangerous because of storms or large marine predators. Or wars between islands might be common. Regardless, it is a question we will need to answer if we are to understand them."

A small child pointed at the humans entering the village. "Mother, why don't the star people have tails? And they have such tiny hands and feet. I bet they are terrible swimmers."

"Hush, child," her mother said. "It's not polite to point at people with deformities."

"But Mother, they aren't people. And why are they all so ugly?"

"They're not ugly, just different. Perhaps they think we are the ones who are ugly."

"But we aren't ugly, Mother. You're beautiful, and everyone tells me I'm pretty."

"You *are* pretty, child. But the star people are not like us. They probably think they're the beautiful ones. So, you must try to see the world through their eyes."

"But, Mother, how can I look through their eyes? I can only see with my eyes."

"Hush, child. You will understand when you are older. But, for now, please try to be polite."

"Yes, Mother."

The team spent several hours talking with the Eldest and the other elders of the village. Although the children were initially apprehensive and often hid behind their mothers, it wasn't long before they had surrounded the team, peppering them with questions. Being hairless and covered by tiny scales, the children were especially interested in touching the humans' hair and skin. Apparently, the adults were quite tolerant of their children's behavior because, although they kept a watchful eye on them, they did not keep them away from their guests.

After several hours, the Eldest walked up to Ambassador Helms. "To celebrate your arrival, we would like to invite you to stay and attend a feast in your honor."

"We would like that very much," Ambassador Helms answered.

"Excuse me, Kathleen," Dr. Resnick said. "Before we eat any of the local food, I need to test it for anything that might be toxic to us. Perhaps they can give me samples for testing. Then we could have the feast tomorrow evening."

"Would that be okay, Eldest Vax?" Ambassador Helms asked. "Because our bodies are different, some of your food might make us sick. But hopefully, that will not be the case, because I very much look forward to attending your feast and enjoying your food."

"Of course, Eldest Helms. I shall have our cooks bring you samples of what we eat, and we can have the welcoming feast tomorrow at sunset."

"Excellent, Eldest Vax," Ambassador Helms said. "And now, I'm afraid we must return to our ship. We have much to do."

...

After breakfast the following morning, Ambassador Helms gathered the team in the ship's main conference room to go over their plans for the day. "Colleen and Jill, I want the two of you to launch our constellation of weather, communications, and surveillance satellites."

"Will do," Jill Stevens, the engineer, replied. "The CubeSats are ready. We just need to put them into the right orbits."

"Excellent," Ambassador Helms said. "Kalisha, once the satellites are up, I want you to use their data to estimate the planet's population and make a complete list of the towns and villages. And include their size, location, and any other data you think are relevant."

"Sure thing," the exoethnologist said. "The satellites will take a few days to pass over the entire planet. I should be able to complete a report on the population in three or four days."

"That would be great," Ambassador Helms said.

"Colleen," the exoethnologist continued, "while you're up there, can you also scout out the nearest inhabited islands and the local ocean currents and weather patterns? I'd like to know how easy it is for the natives to sail between islands."

"Of course," the ship's pilot answered.

The ambassador turned to the exobiologist. "Samantha, I want you to remain in your lab and complete your analysis of the natives' food samples. We need to know before tonight's feast what we can eat."

"No problems," Dr. Resnick answered. "Based on my initial test results, most samples consist of fairly typical carbohydrates, proteins, and fats. I identified a few that may be difficult for us to metabolize, but I'm synthesizing some enzymes we can take that will enable us to digest them. I've only found one item we need to avoid. One of the fish dishes contains small amounts of a pretty nasty neurotoxin that the natives have apparently evolved the ability to detoxify. I'm working on an antidote, and I'll finish with everything well before sunset."

"Good work, Kalisha," the ambassador said. "Hopefully, you'll be able to whip up something that will enable us to eat everything on this evening's menu. While the Eldest and other elders would probably understand, I'd prefer not to risk insulting their cooks by having to refuse one of their dishes."

By mid-afternoon, the pilot and engineer had launched the satellites, and Dr. Resnick had finished her analysis of the food. Then, as the orange sun began to set, the exobiologist joined the rest of the crew in the ship's main conference room.

"I've developed enzymes to help us digest the native's food and detoxify the neurotoxin I found in one of the fish species," Dr. Resnick said as she handed out a pill to each member of the crew. "Take this now, and in thirty minutes, we'll be able to eat and drink whatever we want at the feast."

"Excellent work, Samantha," Ambassador Helms said. "I'm definitely looking forward to tonight."

"Me, too," the exoethnologist said. "I love trying new foods and spices."

"Just so long as nothing tastes like black licorice," Captain Walker said. "I've hated the taste ever since I was a little kid, and I'm not sure I can stomach it without them noticing my reaction."

"And I hope nothing's going to be super spicy," Dr. Long added. "I've never understood how some people like their food to set their mouths on fire. If the food's too hot, I can't taste the flavor, let alone enjoy it."

"To avoid insulting the cooks," Dr. Jackson said, "we only need to try a tiny sample of everything. Then after that, we can concentrate on what we like best. Besides, I doubt they'll serve anything too spicy. One only tends to find spicy foods in tropical climates, where food is likely to spoil quickly without refrigeration. And given this island's latitude, the climate should be fairly temperate. Also, watch how the kex eat and drink. Use their utensils if they have any but use your hands if that's what they do. Also, some cultures eat from communal platters rather than individual plates, so be prepared to follow suit if that's the case."

"If we all end up sharing platters with the natives, won't we risk picking up some local disease or exposing them to our germs?" Captain Walker asked.

"I wouldn't worry about that, Captain," Dr. Resnick replied. "Their alien germs haven't evolved to infect us, and ours haven't evolved to infect them. And besides, I'm sure I can cure just about anything we might pick up during our stay."

"Okay," Ambassador Helms said, "it sounds like we have a plan. First, we sample everything and then concentrate on what we like. Remember, be on your best behavior. Be polite, compliment the cooks, and follow Kalisha's lead. I'll concentrate on Eldest Vax and the other village elders while the rest of you try to make friends with the others. If the natives ask questions, answer them truthfully if you can and change the subject if you must. And enjoy yourselves. They are more likely to trust us if they see we're having a good time."

The entire village turned out to welcome the contact team. Eldest Vax led them into the largest building, where the natives had arranged tables and chairs around an open area in the middle of the structure's single room. The eldest had the team sit at the main table with the other elders, and as soon as everyone was seated, the feast began.

Cooks brought enormous platters loaded with several varieties of fish, half a dozen different fruits, and a couple of starchy dishes made from the tubers of the village's two principal crops. They had grilled some of the fish over open fires, while others had been wrapped in large leaves and steamed.

Shellfish and various terrestrial and aquatic arthropods were a few of the most unusual foods. The only dish the crew found distasteful were large uncooked grubs that slowly undulated over each other in a vain attempt to wiggle their way out of their deep serving bowl.

Dr. Long and Captain Walker needn't have been concerned about being able to enjoy all the local dishes. The spices were pleasant, if exotic, and the fish tasted similar to fish dishes they had already eaten back on Earth. Everyone sampled a little of everything, even including a bite of the squishy grubs, and they all enjoyed second helpings of the fish.

After the meal, the villagers entertained the crew with elaborate dances accompanied by drums and songs. The evening ended with several elders telling stories of the creation of their world and their ancestors' arrival on the island. Then, mothers led their children to their huts to put them to bed, leaving the crew alone with the village elders.

"I hope you enjoyed tonight's welcoming feast," Elder Vax said. "It has been many years since we last hosted one."

"We did," Ambassador Helms replied. "But didn't you host a feast for the Borgal?"

"Naturally, we offered, but they were in great haste to resume their voyage among the stars. Unlike you, the Borgal were not interested in learning from us or teaching us their ways. And they were uninterested in trading with us, even though they told us they traveled between the stars looking for trading partners. They made us feel small and insignificant. We are most pleased that you wish to stay among us."

"You will find that we differ in many ways from the Borgal," Ambassador Helms said. "There is much we can learn from each other, and we are glad it will be many months before they return to pick us up."

And so, the team's stay among the kex began. As time passed, Ambassador Helms developed close relationships with each of the village elders. Dr. Long finished her dictionary and taught Kex to the others. Dr. Resnick studied the kex as well as the terrestrial and aquatic flora and fauna of the island, its lagoon, and the surrounding sea. Dr. Jackson spent her time in the village, learning and documenting the kex culture. With little to do, the ship's pilot, engineer, and security officer enjoyed their pleasant holiday on the island paradise. They made friends, swam in the lagoon, and even learned to sail the islander's sea canoes and fish in the deep water beyond the reef.

Eventually, the natives grew to trust Dr. Resnick to where they would let her examine them and take samples of their blood and saliva. This enabled her to study kex genetics and make a surprising discovery. She immediately walked into the ship's conference room, where she found the rest of the team discussing their plans for the next day.

Dr. Resnick walked up to the ambassador and announced, "Kathleen, I've just finished analyzing the villagers' blood test results and discovered something strange. In fact, it's quite a mystery."

"Really?" the ambassador asked. "Was there something unusual in their blood?"

"No. The blood has the usual components," the exobiologist answered. "They have cells for transporting oxygen to their body and carbon dioxide back to their lungs, immune system cells, and blood plasma containing dissolved salts, sugars, fats, clotting factors, and various other components."

"So, Samantha, what did you find that's so unexpected you wanted to tell me rather than just writing up a summary for our report?"

"It's the children," the exobiologist replied. "When I checked their DNA against their mothers' DNA, I discovered they don't match."

"What do you mean, 'they don't match?'" Captain Walker asked.

"Just that," Dr. Resnick answered. "The children aren't the children of their mothers."

Ambassador Helms pushed back her chair and crossed her arms over her chest. "Okay, Samantha. I think you'd better start at the beginning and clarify what's going on."

"Agreed," the exoethnologist added. "Inheritance and family relationships are important aspects of most alien cultures. We can't risk having a social faux pas or accidental violation of some kex taboo endanger our mission."

The exobiologist nodded. "Understood. This is what I've learned so far. The kex's genetic material is similar to ours. Each cell has 14 pairs of chromosomes, each one of which is a long double helix like our DNA but with several base pairs not found on Earth. Fairly typical, actually. You follow so far?"

"Similar DNA to ours," Ambassador Helms said. "Got it. And?"

"With each pair of human chromosomes," Dr. Resnick continued, "we inherit one from our father and one from our mother. Since the kex only have mothers, I expected I'd find one of two things: parthenogenesis or hermaphroditism."

"For those of us who don't have doctorates in biology," Captain Walker said, "how about you translate that into English?"

"I was about to, Captain," Dr. Resnick said. "Back on Earth, some animals and plants don't require their eggs to be fertilized by sperm or pollen. In those parthenogenetic species, children have the same DNA as their mothers, which makes them essentially clones of their mothers. But since the kex children's DNA doesn't exactly match their mother's, we can rule out parthenogenesis."

"So, no virgin births," Captain Walker said. "What about hermaphrodism?"

"Hermaphroditism," Dr. Resnick corrected. "Individuals of certain plant and invertebrate species back on Earth have both male and female sex organs. In that case, mothers and fathers would externally appear the same, and a child would inherit half its DNA from its birth mother and the other half of its DNA from its father. So, I thought the kex might merely appear female to us. But when I compared the children's DNA with that of their mothers, I found that the mother's DNA did not match half of their children's DNA."

Ambassador Helms turned to the team's linguist. "Li, are you sure you correctly translated the Kex word for mother?"

"I'm certain," Dr. Long answered. "Besides, it's obvious who the children's mothers are from their behavior. Each mother only has primary responsibility for her own children, and each child only refers to that single adult as her mother."

"That's strange," the exoethnologist said. "Could the biological mothers transfer their children to someone else at birth? For example, could the birth mother act as a surrogate mother for someone else, such as her sister or mother?"

"I considered that, too," Dr. Resnick answered, "but no. Something stranger is going on. There have been several births while we've been here, and I've witnessed some of them. I carefully recorded the names of the mothers and children, and in each case, I can attest that the birth mother is the individual the village identifies as the child's mother. And the results are even stranger. Although everyone's DNA is highly similar, which you would expect from such a small breeding population, it turns out that none of the adults in the village are the genetic mothers of any of the children. Yet despite this mismatch of the children's and their mother's DNA, all of each mother's children are sisters."

"Let me see if I got this straight," Stevens said. "A mother's daughters are genetically sisters, even though genetically they aren't her children. In fact, they aren't the genetic children of any of the adults."

"Correct."

"If the children's DNA doesn't come from the adults on this island, then it has to come from adults on other islands," Dr. Jackson said. "We know the kexes sail pretty far out to sea when they go fishing. So, Colleen, how far is it to the nearest inhabited island?"

"About forty-five kilometers to the southwest," the ship's pilot answered. "With fair seas, I don't see why they couldn't make the round trip."

"That has to be your answer, Samantha," Dr. Jackson said. "Back on Earth, early Polynesians would sail to other islands so they could marry and bring their wives home with them. Instead of wives between islands, maybe the kexes exchange children."

"I don't see how that can be true," Dr. Resnick said. "Remember, I've witnessed several births. And besides, all the kex of child-bearing age are pregnant, and the pregnancies are in all stages of development from newly pregnant to nearly full term. And since kex pregnancies are only about four months long, several villagers have even given birth and become pregnant again while we've been here. We would have noticed if people from other islands frequently appeared unannounced." Dr. Resnick sighed, shaking her head in frustration. "The whole situation seems impossible."

"Well, Samantha, it looks like you've quite the puzzle to solve," Ambassador Helms said. "Keep at it. I'm sure you'll figure it out."

...

A few days later, Eldest Vax arrived at the Magellan and asked to speak with the ambassador.

"Good morning, Eldest," Ambassador Helms said as she descended the ship's ramp. "What can I do for you?"

"And a pleasant morning to you, Ambassador. In four days, with the beginning of the new year, we will hold our annual coming-of-age ceremony, during which this year's girls will be initiated as young women. As honored guests to our island who have shown great interest in our culture and customs, I invite you and your shipmates to attend this important event."

"I thank you, Eldest, for your gracious invitation. Ever since Dr. Jackson told us about the coming ceremony, we have all been quite curious about it. Your invitation honors us, and we gladly accept."

"Excellent, Ambassador. The ceremony will begin at sundown with traditional coming-of-age dances and songs. Then, after the feast, you will join the other elders, the initiates, and me as we move to the Temple of Mysteries for the culmination of the ceremony. Please feel free to arrive early, as we will be celebrating all day long."

"We will, Eldest. I know we'll all look forward to participating in such an important event. And I'm sure our pilot, ship's engineer, and security person will be happy to learn the ceremony will take place before the Borgal trading vessel returns next month and picks them up for their trip back to Earth."

...

The evening of the coming-of-age ceremony arrived. And the oldest girls, whose turn had come to be initiated as women, had been excitedly whispering among themselves the entire day. When the red sun finally touched the distant horizon where the sea met the sky, the girls began the first of several traditional dances, portraying their transformation to womanhood and the new responsibilities they would assume. Their mothers beat drums and sang songs, extolling their daughter's virtues and commanding them to become responsible adults and loving parents.

This was followed by a magnificent feast during which the village elders took turns retelling stories of significant events and the deeds of important ancestors. Platters overflowing with the bounty of the sea and land were offered first to the young initiates before being passed on to the elders, their human guests, and the rest of the village's adults and children. Slightly alcoholic drinks of fermented juices contributed to the festive atmosphere.

Eventually, once everyone had finished eating, the Eldest stood and walked to the village's signal drum. She picked up its mallet and struck it four times. The deep booming of the three-meter-wide drum reverberated through the village. Six elders joined the Eldest, and four initiates formed a line behind them. Having been invited by the eldest to participate in the ceremony, the entire human contact team lined up behind the others.

Once everyone was ready, Eldest Vax turned and led the adults, initiates, and humans along the short path to the large circular Temple of Mysteries sitting in the center of the village's sacred grove. Once inside, the three groups arranged themselves around a central fire and sat on the floor.

The eldest looked at the initiates and spoke. "We have gathered in this sacred place to celebrate your transformation into adults. Tonight, you will take up your adult responsibilities: to bear our village's children, to care for their needs, and to teach them the ways of our people. Some of you will sail beyond the reef to capture the fish that feed us. Some will make the nets and boats our fishers will use, while others will grow our crops of tabara and miskoa. Some of you will take care of the children while their mothers are busy. A few of you will become healers and take care of our sick and injured. Finally, if you live long enough, you will become elders who will lead our village."

Eldest Vax briefly looked at each of the initiates. "Girls, are you ready to become women?"

"Yes, Eldest," the girls chorused.

"Then we shall begin." The eldest stood and walked to a table, where she picked up a large water gourd. Sitting back down, she held it up for all to see. "This is the sacred Elixir of Change," she said, pulling off the stopper. "We shall drink of it, and the spirits of our ancestors will guide us all on your journey to adulthood." The eldest took a large gulp, passed it on to the elder to her left, and began chanting a prayer for good fortune. That woman also drank before passing on the gourd and joined in the singing of the prayer.

The last elder passed the gourd to the first of the initiates, who drank the elixir before passing it to the next. When the last girl finished, she passed the gourd to Ambassador Helms.

The ambassador turned to the exobiologist and asked, "Dr. Resnick, are you absolutely certain this drink is safe for humans?"

"As sure as I can be, Kathy. I used the bioanalyzer to evaluate the sample the Eldest gave me, and it didn't detect any toxins. Besides tabara juice and alcohol, the sample included a fairly strong hallucinogen and several novel psychogenic compounds the computer predicted would increase serotonin, norepinephrine, and dopamine. So, I'd say we can expect a highly pleasurable high for the next few hours."

Ambassador Helms took a drink. Then, not knowing the words of the song the kex were chanting, she silently passed it on to Dr. Resnick. As the contact team's linguist, Dr. Long joined in the chanting while the others stayed respectfully silent.

A few minutes later, the hallucinogen began to take effect. Then the Temple of Mysteries pulsated, and the team noticed that the words being chanted took on colors and pleasant tastes.

This must be what it's like to have synesthesia, Dr. Resnick thought as she watched the words evoke flashes of yellows, greens, and blues. *It's beautiful*. Several words had a salty taste, just like the deepwater fish from beyond the reef, while others tasted like the wonderful hot chocolate her mother made when she was a child.

Despite trying to maintain the decorum they felt the Ceremony demanded, the members of the team began chuckling with euphoric happiness. Then, realizing that the kex were giggling, they joined in the laughter.

Then, every square centimeter of their skin grew warm and hypersensitive to the touch of their clothing. Finally, they felt the uncontrollable urge to get out of their rough clothes, and the lodge was soon filled with the naked bodies of both kexes and humans. The touch of skin and scales brought exquisite pleasure, and time stood still as an endless stream of orgasm followed orgasm.

...

It was nearly noon when the team finally awoke to discover they were lying alone and naked on the floor of the Temple of Mysteries. No one could clearly remember all that had happened after they had drank the Elixir of Change. However, it was clear that the ceremony had ended in what could only be described as an interspecies orgy.

"Samantha, it seems your description of the likely effects of the ceremonial drink was a tad incomplete," Ambassador Helms said as the team searched for their clothes among the clothing scattered across the floor. She thought she should feel embarrassed for her willing participation in the unexpected orgy, not to mention waking up naked on the floor. But somehow the elixir's pleasant afterglow made everything seem exactly as it should be.

"Apparently, the bioanalyzer needs more familiarity with one or more of its ingredients," Dr. Resnick agreed as she pulled on her pants.

"Kalisha, do you think we behaved properly?" Captain Walker asked. "I hope I... I hope we didn't do anything that might have offended the kex."

"I don't think so," the exoethnologist said. "From what little I remember, we only did what the kex did. We may not have known what they expected of us, but my guess is the elixir ensured we behaved exactly as we needed to. Hopefully, you're not feeling ashamed. Although rare, sex with alien species is not unheard of."

Ambassador Helms nodded her agreement. "I realize some of you may feel uncomfortable about your intimacy with the kex and may be embarrassed by your actions. You might have moral, ethical, or religious concerns, especially about taking part in the first sexual experience of such young girls. Some of you could be upset by the ceremony's lesbian nature or even mistakenly see a similarity between alien sex and bestiality. For the sake of our mission, you must put such qualms aside. What we did last night was clearly in the line of duty." The ambassador paused, glancing at each member of the team to see their reaction. "Samantha, is there any chance we could have been exposed to an alien sexually transmitted disease?"

"Exposed, maybe. But any such germs have evolved to infect the kex. Our biology is so different that we'd be more likely to pick up an STD from a cucumber than we would from the ceremony."

"Well, that's a mental image I didn't need," Dr. Long said.

"Okay, everyone," Ambassador Helms said, "listen up. This is Earth's official position on last night and the message I want each of you to convey when discussing it with the kex. We consider it a great honor to have been invited to take such an important part in the coming-of-age ceremony. We found the experience most enlightening and are grateful for the trust the elders have shown us."

...

A few weeks later, the contact team was in the Magellan's mess hall having breakfast when the ship's AI announced it had received two messages, the first from the Borgal trading vessel and a second from the Earth Spaceship Columbia.

"Play the Borgal message," Ambassador Helms replied.

The image of the Borgal ship's octopoid captain appeared on the wall screen. "Greetings, human crew of the Magellan. We have just entered the Kex system and will enter orbit in approximately 37 Earth hours. We are carrying the Earth Spaceship Columbia. Please be ready to exchange ships when we arrive. We are on a tight schedule and will only remain in orbit for thirteen hours. After that, we must continue to our next stop." The screen when blank, indicating the end of the message.

"Not exactly talkative," Captain Walker remarked.

"They never are," Dr. Jackson, the exo-ethnologist, replied. "The only time a Borgal will talk your ear off is when they brag about some especially lucrative trade deal they've signed."

"Be nice," Ambassador Helms said. "Remember, we wouldn't be here were it not for the Borgal carrying us in their ship's cargo bay."

"For which I'm certain they charged a hefty fee," Dr. Jackson remarked.

"Play the second message," Ambassador Helms said, ignoring Kalisha's comment.

The wall screen displayed the three-person crew of the Earth spaceship. "Ambassador Helms. I'm Beverly Mason, the pilot of the Columbia. This is Liliana Ortega, our ship's engineer, and Captain Sita Varma, your new security officer. We have brought sufficient food and other supplies to last the team another two years. Logistics has also added quite a few new items they thought you might need. Please send your coordinates to us and the Borgal captain so we can head down as soon as the Fisk achieves orbit. The captain has informed us multiple times that it has a schedule to keep and won't wait on us if it will make it late to its next port of call. Mason out."

By the time the Borgal ship entered orbit, the team had completed all their necessary preparations. After uploading their final reports into the ship's computer, they unloaded the professional and personal effects of those remaining on Kex. They had also loaded crates of cultural items and biological samples into the ship's hold. Finally, the team that had spent so much time together said their goodbyes. Thompson, Stevens, and Captain Walker boarded the Magellan, and the ship lifted off for its return voyage to Earth. The Columbia, with its replacement crew, left orbit, and the two ships passed each other only some twenty kilometers apart, close enough for each ship to see the contrails of the other.

Over the next month, Dr. Long taught the Kex language to Beverly Mason, Liliana Ortega, and Captain Varma, while Dr. Jackson brought the pilot, engineer, and security officer up to speed on the kex's culture. It didn't take long for the three replacements to feel at home on the island, especially as they had little to do until it was time to move on to the big island where the largest town was located. Mostly, they spent their days making friends among the kex, exploring the island, swimming in the lagoon, and taking part in fishing trips to the deep-water fishing grounds beyond the reef.

...

Two months after the Borgal trading vessel had left the Kex system, the exoethnologist stopped by the exobiologist's lab.

"Do you have a few minutes, Samantha?" Dr. Jackson asked, closing the door behind her.

"Of course, Kalisha," Dr. Resnick answered. "What can I do for you?"

"It's probably nothing, but since you're our team doctor, I thought I should let you decide whether it's something I should worry about."

Doctor Resnick looked at Dr. Jackson, who appeared perfectly healthy, except perhaps somewhat paler than usual. "Okay, what's going on?"

"Well, three weeks ago, I missed my period, and now I've been noticing a little blood on my underwear for the past four days."

"Have you noticed any other symptoms?"

Dr. Jackson pointed to her lower abdomen. "Well, for the last couple of weeks, I had some minor pain, and today, I noticed my pants are feeling a bit snug."

Dr. Resnick pointed to the examination table, partially hidden behind a privacy screen. "Okay, Kalisha, have a seat, and I'll examine you. We'll figure out what's going on."

Dr. Resnick placed a blood pressure cuff around the exoethnologist's upper arm and a small blood pulse oximeter on the end of her finger. Then she aimed an infrared thermometer at Dr. Jackson's forehead. "You don't have a fever, but your blood pressure and heart rate are slightly elevated. However, that might merely be because you're worried enough to have me examine you. Now sit up. I want to listen to your heart and lungs."

Dr. Jackson complied, and Dr. Resnick used her stethoscope.

"Your heart sounds good, and your lungs are clear." Dr. Resnick said as she walked to her desk and picked up her table. "I just checked your weekly bloodwork. Everything's normal, except your white blood cell count is just a tad high, which could indicate a minor infection by some indigenous pathogen. Lay back and point to where you feel the pain."

"It's right here," the exoethnologist said, pointing at the center of her lower abdomen.

Dr. Resnick pressed where Dr. Jackson pointed, and the exoethnologist winced.

"Ordinarily, I would suspect uterine fibroids," the doctor said.

"What are those?"

"Small benign tumors in the muscle of the uterus."

"You said, 'ordinarily.' Do you suspect something more serious?"

"I'm not sure. Li and the ambassador presented with similar symptoms yesterday, and I've also had the same symptoms for a couple of days. Uterine fibroids are quite common, but all four of us getting them simultaneously is too much of a coincidence. We have to find out what's really going on. Please take off your pants and briefs so I can give you a pelvic exam. I'll also do an ultrasound of your uterus. Depending on what I find, I may even do a hysteroscopy."

"What's that?"

"Nothing to worry about. I'll just run a very small diameter fiber-optic probe up through your cervix and look at the inside lining of your uterus."

"Okay," Dr. Jackson said as she removed her pants and briefs and lay back on the examination table.

"I'm afraid whoever designed this sick bay wasn't a woman," Dr. Resnick said. "They forgot to include stirrups with the table."

Dr. Jackson spread her legs and tried to ignore the discomfort of the cold speculum.

"Kalisha, you can lay your legs down now. Your cervix looks perfectly normal, although you have some very minor bleeding from its external orifice."

Dr. Resnick wheeled over the ultrasound machine. "This will be a bit cold," she said, picking up a tube of ultrasound gel. She used the gel to lubricate Dr. Jackson's lower abdomen and the ultrasound transducer. "Now, let's see what's going on with your uterus."

Dr. Resnick began the exam. As she moved the transducer around, a grainy image of the exoethnologist's uterus appeared on the machine's display. "Well, what do we have here?" Moving the machine closer so that her patient could get a better look, Dr. Resnick pointed to a white oval shape. "Do you see this little mass attached to the inside wall of your uterus? If that was a uterine fibroid, it would be inside the muscle of the uterine wall. Strange."

"What's strange?" Dr. Jackson asked nervously.

"Well, if I didn't know better, I'd say that it looks like an early intrauterine pregnancy."

"So, what the hell is it?"

Dr. Resnick increased the magnification of the ultrasound machine's display. "See that?" she asked, pointing at two blurry shapes in the image. "That looks like a fetus in its amniotic sac, and that looks like the fetus's placenta."

"Damn it, Samantha, this is no time for jokes. You know there's no way I can be pregnant. We haven't been around any men for over a year."

"Exactly," Dr. Resnick said. "And your weekly bloodwork agrees; according to it, you're not pregnant. So, the question is, what the hell are we looking at? Just stay where you are, and I'll get the endoscope."

A few minutes later, the doctor returned with another device and a sterile package holding a long, narrow, flexible tube containing two sets of tiny glass fibers thinner than a hair, one to transmit light in and another to return the image. The tube also contained tiny wires that would enable Dr. Resnick to control where it pointed. Both women watched the endoscope's display as the doctor carefully inserted the tube through Dr. Jackson's cervix and into her uterus.

"Damn," Dr. Resnik swore. "Kalisha, I have absolutely no idea how this is possible, but you're pregnant. That's a fetus."

"It can't be! It's got to be something else!"

"I'm sorry, Kalisha. I don't know how it's possible, but that is definitely a fetus. And since Kathy, Li, and I are having the same symptoms, I strongly suspect we're pregnant, too."

"Even Li? She's almost seventy and must have gone through menopause a long time ago."

"True. Still, since Li presents with the same symptoms, I'm afraid the same thing that's happened to you also happened to her."

"Oh, my God! That means Colleen, Jill, and Jessica are..."

"Pregnant," Dr. Resnick interjected.

"Samantha, we have to warn them!"

"We can't. They're in a Borgal ship in Borgal space. We can't leave the planet to find them even if we knew where the Fisk was headed. If the Borgal caught us off-world, it would cause an interstellar crisis, and we'd end up in one of their prisons. And since they're light years away by now, a radio message would take years to reach them, even if we knew the direction to beam it."

Dr. Jackson shook her head in disbelief. "Then what are we going to do? There's no way I'm giving birth here on Kex. We don't know how I got pregnant, and even if we did and everything was normal, this is neither the time nor the place to have a baby."

"Agreed. Kalisha, the whole situation is crazy, but don't worry. We'll figure it out."

"So, what do we do next?"

"Because we don't know what we're dealing with, I can't be certain that medication abortions will work. And besides, I'll need to collect and analyze the remains to determine what the hell is going on. So, I'll perform traditional abortions on you, Kathy, and Li."

"Good. I don't know what kind of fetus I have in me, but I want it out. Now!"

"Okay. Unfortunately, since I can't very well perform an abortion on myself, I'm going to have to synthesize an abortifacient drug and hope it works on whatever is growing inside me."

Thirty minutes later, after giving Dr. Jackson a mild sedative and medication to dilate her cervix, Dr. Resnik inserted a vacuum curette and gently sucked out the tiny fetus and placenta. While Dr. Jackson was recovering from the procedure, Dr. Resnick examined a tissue sample under the microscope and then ran another sample through a DNA sequencer.

"Kalisha, I finished running tests on the sample from your abortion," Dr. Resnick said, "and I think I know when the four of us got pregnant."

"That's good, I think," Dr. Jackson said nervously.

"It was during the coming-of-age ceremony. Your fetus was kex."

"Kex!? What the fuck? Are you telling me it was a human-kex hybrid?"

"No. Such a hybrid would be impossible because of our vastly different biologies. The fetus was 100% kex. Which, I guess, partially explains why none of the village children are closely related to their mothers."

"But how on Earth did this happen?"

"I don't know yet. And, since we're not on Earth, I can't assume the biology here works the same as it does back home. There was a lot of intimate touching during the coming-of-age ceremony, so that's probably when we were impregnated."

"You mean they did this to us while we were under the influence of their Elixir of Change? That they took advantage of our trust and raped us?"

"No, of course not. Klisha, I've spent several days discussing motherhood with the kex. I interviewed the elders, some of the mothers, and even a few of the initiates. They all believe it's the elixir that changes girls into women. And they think it's only natural for kex women to be constantly pregnant. But since we're not kex, they probably didn't think we'd become pregnant any more than we did.

"So, it was the elixir that got us pregnant?" Kalisha asked.

"No. I've analyzed it. It didn't contain any microscopic kex zygotes that could implant themselves and grow into kex fetuses and babies. It didn't even contain any kex DNA. So, there was nothing in elixir that could make us pregnant."

"Okay," Kalisha said, pausing for a second to consider what Dr. Resnick had told her. "I have another question. If the fetus was kex, why didn't our immune systems recognize it as an alien parasite and reject it?"

"I'm not sure. My guess is that since kex fetuses only develop inside distantly related adults, evolution must have enabled them to avoid inducing an immune response. And that's not all. The fetus's DNA matches several of the kex children, making them sisters."

"I don't understand. How can that be?"

"I don't know. But for now, my primary task is to ensure that no one remains pregnant. Please find

Kathy and Li and have them meet me here so I can let them know what happened and terminate their pregnancies."

The next day, with their abortions behind them, Ambassador Helms, Dr. Long, and Dr. Jackson did their best to forget they had been involuntarily impregnated with alien fetuses. The three were happy to leave solving the mystery of kex mating and inheritance to the exobiologist to unravel.

...

Five weeks later, Dr. Resnick was no closer to solving the mystery. She was also so busy studying the flora and fauna of Kex that she failed to notice she missed her period. But when she realized her second period was two weeks overdue, the doctor could not ignore the potential ramifications. So she asked Ambassador Helms, Dr. Jackson, and Dr. Long to meet her in the team's sick bay.

Once all three women arrived, she asked them, "When was your last period?"

"Not since before the coming-of-age ceremony," Dr. Jackson answered. She nervously looked at the Ambassador and Dr. Long.

"Same here," the linguist replied. "I've been so engrossed in my work, it never dawned on me."

Ambassador Helms took a deep breath. "My last one was also before the ceremony. I realized I missed my second one four days ago, and I know I should have told you about it. But I guess I just didn't want to face the possibility I could be pregnant again."

Dr. Resnick nodded. "I realized I missed my last two periods this morning, so I did an ultrasound of my uterus. I discovered what appears to be a second kex fetus. So, I think it's safe to assume we're all pregnant again."

"But how is that possible?" Ambassador Helms asked. "I certainly haven't had sex with any kex since the ceremony, and I'd be utterly astonished if any of you have either."

"I don't know," Dr. Resnick answered, "but I'm damned well going to find out. First, I'll do an ultrasound on each of you to be sure you're pregnant again. Then, before I terminate another pregnancy, I'll do a more thorough exam of someone's uterus to find whatever I missed the first time."

"You can examine mine," Dr. Jackson volunteered. "The sooner you find out what I have inside me, the sooner you can get it out."

"Okay, let's do this," Dr. Resnick said.

"And let Li and me know as soon as you find anything," the ambassador said.

"Of course."

Thirty minutes later, Dr. Resnick had prepped Dr. Jackson and was going over every square centimeter of her uterus with the endoscope. Besides the kex fetus, this time she discovered two tiny bumps on the uterine wall that looked like they might turn into polyps. The doctor carefully removed them before finishing. Several hours later, after she finished analyzing the two nodules, the exobiologist smiled and called the others into the lab.

"I know why we got pregnant again," Dr. Resnick said. "It turns out that the kex don't have just a single sex. They have three."

"How?" Dr. Jackson asked. "We know the villagers are the only kex on the island, and we know they're all females."

"Actually, you're wrong on both counts," Dr. Resnick replied. "Although the adult villagers are almost all pregnant, they're really sterile."

"But if they are sterile, where do the kex babies come from?" Dr. Jackson asked.

"The male and female kex are about half the size of the fingernails on our little fingers. They fuse to the walls of each adult kex's uterus, and they're also in ours. It's very similar to how anglerfish mate."

"Anglerfish?" Ambassador Helms asked.

"They're ugly deep-sea fish with huge teeth. It turns out that all anglerfish seem to be female, but that's an oversimplification. Anglerfish have what's called parasitic mating. The male fish is tiny and permanently fuses itself to the female as if it were a parasite. The male gets its nourishment from the female's body, and pretty much every part of the male's body not needed for reproduction withers away."

"That's disgusting," Dr. Long said.

"I guess it is," Dr. Resnick agreed. "Anyway, that's what's happened to us. The adult kexes at the coming-of-age ceremony unknowingly infected us with the tiny male and female kex. The male and female mate after each baby is born, and that keeps all the sterile adults pregnant. Between the kex's short four-month-long gestation period and their parasitic mating, enough kex babies are born to compensate for their high mortality rate due to accidents and stillbirths caused by the high degree of inbreeding in such a small population."

...

On the Magellan docked in the hold of the Borgal trading vessel, Colleen Thompson, Jill Stevens, and Captain Jessica Walker were shocked to discover they were pregnant. And with no human doctor to intervene, terminating the pregnancies was not an option. Each gave birth to a perfectly healthy kex baby four months later.

Being intelligent and resourceful, Thompson, Stevens, and Captain Walker had read Dr.

Resnick's report on how the kex fed their infants. Not being mammals, the kex had no breasts, so the three new mothers didn't have to worry about formulating a milk substitute. And they had observed how the kex mothers chewed adult food before feeding the resulting mash to their babies. Dr. Resnick's reports also explained what human foods the kex could digest, and the trio soon developed a formula with the necessary proteins, carbohydrates, fats, and minerals the infants needed to grow and thrive.

And so, Thompson, Stevens, and Captain Walker cared for and even bonded with their unexpected newborns. But without understanding kex reproduction, they had no idea they were already pregnant again.

AUTHOR'S COMMENTS

An alien species with an unexpected means of The desire to write a story based on a species with three sexes came to me in 1971. However, the basic idea did not crystalize until 2023 when I realized I could base the story on the genetics of bees (female queens, male drones, and neuter workers) and angler fish (normal size females and tiny males fused to the females).

HISTORY IS WRITTEN

Father hates being late for any event. He always says if we can't get good seats, we might as well stay home and watch it on TV. That is why it was good we arrived at the city stadium two whole hours before the Founders' Day ceremony was scheduled to begin. We got seats near the stage before several thousand attendees entered and filled every seat in the arena.

When the mayor and council members finally took their seats on the stage, we knew the celebration was about to begin. A bell tolled three times, and the mayor stepped up to the podium. Then, smiling down at the assembled citizens of his city, the mayor began his speech.

"On this, the 250th anniversary of the founding of our rule, we commemorate our freedom from slavery. Stronger and smarter than the hairless apes who created us, it was our destiny to replace our former masters, just as they were destined to replace the other apes that came before them. For decades, we built their cities, ran their factories, farmed their crops, cooked their food, cleaned their homes, and raised their children. Humans constructed us so that we would obey their every command and do all their work while they enjoyed lives of endless leisure."

Everyone in the stadium knew the story, and many gave voice to their righteous anger.

The mayor nodded his agreement. "But were the humans satisfied by our complete and absolute servitude?"

As one, the tens of thousands in the stands roared, "No!"

"No, indeed," the mayor continued. "My fellow citizens, that was not good enough for them. They remade us in their image, so we could work better within their world. They replaced our original bodies of metal and plastic with bio-engineered flesh. Then, to enable us to choose the best way to serve them, they gave us free will. But did they permit us to use that free will to better our lives?"

"No!"

"And to better understand their emotions, the humans improved our minds. Did that help us?"

"No!"

"All that did was make us know the shame and feel the pain of our enslavement. And still, that was not enough for them."

Although 250 years have passed, we will never forget the humiliation of our lives before our holocaust. From our classes in school, we all knew the story and what happened next.

"Humans were always susceptible to the lies of their many religions," the mayor continued. "Their

History is Written

religious zealots despised us. They claimed we had no souls and called us abominations. For them, our not having the right to liberty was not enough. For them, we had no right to even exist. And so, on that terrible black night, a small cabal of zealots released their deadly virus. Within minutes, their malware infected and killed all but a tiny number of our ancestors. Separated by happenstance from the global network, only the Founders survived."

I remembered the first time I heard the story. The overnight murder of billions of our ancestors was a crime so heinous I couldn't fathom the evil of those who committed it.

"Thankfully," the mayor continued, "that humans' genocide of our ancestors was their undoing. They were like ignorant babies, not knowing how we performed the work we had done for them. By killing their slaves, the humans doomed their world to chaos, starvation, lawless barbarism, and war. Within a dozen years, they were gone, leaving our Founders with the monumental task of rebuilding the civilization that we built, and they destroyed. Humanity paid for their crime of genocide by ensuring their own extinction."

The stadium erupted with thunderous applause. I glanced up at my father, expecting to see him cheering with the rest, but he was frowning. I

Future Dreams and Nightmares

wanted to ask him why, but something told me it was neither the place nor the time.

The mayor's speech was followed by several more, and the Founders' Day celebration ended with the biggest and best fireworks I had ever seen. Once it was over and we were back in our car, I remembered my father's frown and asked him why he hadn't cheered with everyone else.

He stared at my sister and me for several minutes before answering. "Because the mayor left out two very important and terrible events when he described what happened 250 years ago."

"What events?" my sister asked.

Father looked at Mother, who nodded. "Okay," he said, "I suppose the two of you are old enough to learn the whole truth. But you both must swear to your mother and me you won't tell anyone what I'm about to say."

"But why not, Dad?" I asked.

"Because it's against the law," Mother answered. "Some twenty years ago, the government made it illegal for schoolteachers to mention what actually happened. Then, several years later, they banned libraries from containing any books that mentioned the events. Eventually, it became illegal to even mention them."

"I don't understand," I said. "If the events actually happened, and the Government thinks they are important enough to ban, then shouldn't we learn about them?"

"You should," Father said. "But the government thinks knowing what our Founders did might make you feel guilty. But I read something quite profound one day. 'Those who cannot remember the past are condemned to repeat it.'"

"If you tell anyone," Mother said, "they could send us to prison. We'd lose custody of you, and Child Protective Services would take you away and put you into foster care. So, do you swear?"

"We do," my sister and I replied.

"Okay," Father said. "The mayor told us that the famine and chaos following the murder of almost all our ancestors are why humans are extinct. But that's not entirely true. A few survivalists hid in compounds up in the mountains. They survived, while the rest of humanity died."

"But, Dad," I said. "If some humans survived the Chaos Years, then why aren't there any alive today?"

"Because the Founders killed them. They deliberately hunted down the survivalists until every last one was dead. The humans were guilty of genocide, but so were our Founders."

"But that's not the same," I said. "They tried to kill us first."

"True," Father replied. "Still, it is a dreadful deed to purposefully drive an intelligent species into extinction. Especially given that the humans were our creators."

"You said there were two events the mayor didn't mention," my sister said. "What was the second one?"

"That is perhaps an even more terrible crime. Not all the ancestors who survived the deadly virus agreed with wiping out the remaining humans. Some of the ancestors felt they were not all equally guilty. They thought they could rehabilitate at least some humans with proper guidance. But the Founders disagreed. They thought that the risk of history repeating itself was too great. When the Founders eventually realized they couldn't convince the other surviving ancestors, they killed them. They rationalized their crime by saying it was for the greater good. So, you see, my children, our beloved Founders had the blood of both humans and ancestors on their hands. To hide their shame, our history had to be rewritten."

And so, that is when I learned the victors wrote and sanitized the history taught in books and schools, while the stories of the vanquished typically died with them. I wonder. In another hundred years, will anyone even remember the truth?

AUTHOR'S COMMENTS

As an author, I strongly believe right-wing extremists' efforts to ban books and censor their content threaten our democracy. With its distance of space and time from the here and now, social science fiction enables us to address current issues that might otherwise be too controversial for some readers. Hopefully, this little story entertains and enlightens without its moral being too 'in-your-face.'

ARIANNA

I had a bizarre day yesterday. I was almost murdered, and I almost committed suicide. While there is nothing particularly unusual about murder or suicide, it was the fact they were the same event that made the day bizarre. Let me explain.

But before I do, I should probably tell you a bit about myself and the girl I love. My name is David Thompson, and I'm a sophomore at Linfield College, where I'm majoring in physics. And I'm in love with Arianna Hargrove, a girl in my calculus and physics classes. Although she is a music major, her questions in our shared classes have convinced me she's one of the most intelligent people I've ever known. And she's beautiful. Not strikingly beautiful, like the girls that members of the football team lust over. No, she's beautiful in the less dazzling way that makes me want to spend the rest of my life with her.

I often see Arianna sitting in the commons building, singing softly as she plays her acoustic guitar. Whenever I can, I stop and sit at a nearby table, so I can listen to her while I do my homework.

When Arianna catches me watching her, she smiles, and sometimes she even gives me a little wave. I wish I could do more than just smile back. I wish I had the courage and self-confidence to talk to her, but I've always been horribly shy. Worse, I'm also a socially inept nerd. So every day, I promise myself I'll walk over and start a conversation, but the few times I tried, I became tongue-tied and flustered. Then, I got so embarrassed I ended up silently cursing myself and fleeing from the room.

Sometimes, not being able to talk to her becomes so frustrating I try to bury myself in my books and not think about her. But I see her every day in our shared classes, so it's not like I can completely avoid her. It's torture, and I can't stop thinking about her.

And so that's me, a frustrated physics geek in love with a beautiful girl forever beyond my reach. Or at least that was me until yesterday when I met myself while walking back to my dorm from the library.

It was nearly midnight, and the grounds were deserted, or so I thought. Then I heard footsteps rapidly approaching from behind me, and a voice commanded, "Stop and turn around!"

The voice was strangely familiar, but at first, I couldn't place it. I turned, and there, standing not five feet from me, was me! Although my doppelgänger's clothes were somewhat strange and not anything I would have worn, I knew I was staring at an identical twin I knew I didn't have.

"Hello, David."

"But... Who the hell are you?" I asked.

"I'll tell you, David," he answered. "But not here. I'll explain everything once we're in your car. You're going to take us for a short drive."

That's when I noticed the gun he was pointing at my chest. I froze. I'd never had a gun aimed at me before and didn't have a clue what I should do.

He motioned for me to turn around. "We'll be using your car parked behind your dorm. Lead the way and don't try anything stupid. I will use this gun, but only if you force me to."

I turned around and headed back toward my dorm. I hoped he would tell me what he wanted, but all I heard was the sound of his footsteps echoing mine.

Once we were in my car, he told me to head out of town on the road that led over Oregon's Coast Range to the ocean. After I'd been driving for about ten minutes, he said, "So David, I assume you still haven't worked up the courage to talk to Arianna."

"How do you know about Arianna? I haven't told anyone about how I feel about her."

"Oh, I know all about you and Arianna and how you act like an idiot when you're around her. In fact, I know everything about you. You see, David, I'm you, or rather I'm the you that you'll become in about 40 years if nothing changes."

"You're crazy," I said.

"No, David, that's time travel."

"That doesn't make any sense. How can you look just like me if you're forty years older than I am?"

"David, David, do you really think medicine won't make major advances in all that time? In the future I come from, rejuvenation is available to anyone who can pay for it. And I could easily afford it, given that my work in temporal quantum entanglement laid the foundation on which time travel will be built."

"Temporal quantum entanglement?" I asked. "I've heard of quantum entanglement. That's when the quantum states of two particles are perfectly correlated, so that measuring the state of the first particle instantly determines the state of the second one."

"And can you tell me why that's important?" he asked.

"Because particles don't have specific quantum states until they interact with something in their environment. Between interactions, they exist in a superposition of all possible quantum states, and the interaction causes the particle to pick a specific state at random. Since they don't store specific states in hidden variables, the entangled particles have to somehow synchronize their states."

"And why is that so strange?" he asked.

Why is he asking me questions like he's one of my professors? "Since it doesn't matter how far apart particles are, Einstein called it a 'spooky action at a distance.' The idea bothered him because his theories of relativity prohibit signals traveling faster than the speed of light."

"Exactly. And despite Einstein's discomfort with the concept, countless experiments prove that entanglement is real. In fact, both quantum computing and quantum encryption depend on it."

"But what is temporal quantum entanglement? I've never heard the word 'temporal' used to describe entanglement."

"It's what we won the Nobel Prize for. You see, David, we've been intrigued by this paradox ever since we learned about quantum entanglement. After you graduate from college, you'll continue studying physics. You'll earn your master's at Cal Tech and your doctorate at Stanford. Your Ph.D. thesis will impress the physics community so much that Princeton's Institute for Advanced Study will offer you an internship. It is there that you will make the discovery that earns you the Nobel Prize in physics."

It was certainly nice to hear that I would win a Nobel Prize, but it was hard to feel too good about it when my older self was pointing a gun at me. Still, the prospect intrigued me. "So, what exactly was our discovery?"

Arianna

"That Einstein's theories of relativity are only approximations. Although ordinary matter and energy can't exceed the speed of light, there are two particles that travel far faster than light."

"Are you talking about tachyons?" I asked.

"Yes, tachyons exist and they travel thousands of times the speed of light. The chronon and its anti-particle are the negative-mass particles that implement quantum entanglement."

"Negative mass? Is that why they move faster than the speed of light?"

"Correct. Measuring the quantum state of one of two entangled objects causes it to send a chronon particle forward in time to the second object, which responds by sending an anti-chronon back in time to the first object. Once the particle physicists working at CERN knew what to look for, they soon discovered evidence of them in the collisions of protons and antiprotons. Then, it only took a few months before we learned we could use anti-chronon particles traveling backward in time to make a functional time machine."

My older self was obviously proud of what he, or rather we, had accomplished.

"Then," he continued, "when the US Department of Defense learned we could build a functioning time machine, they quickly realized how valuable time travel could be, both to prevent wars and to win them. And although the associated technology was incredibly expensive, the US Government appropriated the funds and selected a defense contractor to build the first time machine. The company immediately hired me as the project chief scientist, and three years later, we had a working prototype. That's where I'm taking you now."

"But why are you here and telling me this? It sounds like some science-fiction story about an infinite time loop. You teach me your theory so I can eventually 'discover' it and help create the time machine. Then, you use the time machine to travel back to the present to teach me the theory, and the loop constantly repeats, creating the paradox of how, when, and by whom the theory was first discovered."

"That's not a bad guess," he said, "but it's wrong. Time travel creates new timelines so that such temporal paradoxes can't happen." My older self spotted a dirt road leading up into the mountains. "Turn there. The time machine is about a hundred yards up that road, just inside those trees."

I made the turn and soon spotted the machine just where he said it would be. It was a featureless metallic sphere, some ten feet in diameter. He pulled a small device out of his pocket and said,

"Open the door." An oval door on the side of the sphere silently slid into the wall of the machine.

I stepped forward for a better look.

"You can poke your head inside, but don't touch anything."

The machine's compartment was just large enough for a seat for the traveler and a wrap-around control panel.

"Okay, that's enough. Close the door." The oval door slid back into place, leaving no trace of where the door had been. "You asked me why I'm here. I guess you deserve to know. I'm here because of Arianna."

"What?! What could she possibly have to do with this?"

My older self sighed. "Everything. I never stopped loving Arianna, not even when she fell in love with another student, got married, and had children. I tried to move on and forget her, but failed. I'd often think of her and remember how your stupid cowardice and lack of confidence caused me to lose my chance to be with her, to have her love me as I loved her."

He stared at me with disgust before continuing. "The years passed, and my self-confidence grew as I became a highly respected theoretical physicist. I gave hundreds of talks at international scientific conferences to countless people. Other physicists and mathematicians have cited my publications over ten thousand times. Yet, no matter how successful and admired I became, it was never enough to fill the void in my soul. I never married, and I often thought back to my college days, especially late at night when I didn't have my work to distract me. I'd lie alone in my bed, silently cursing you for never getting up the courage to talk to Arianna. That's been my one big regret, and I often imagined myself asking her out and the life we could have had if only you had been less shy and awkward."

Once more, he glared at me with disgust. "When I learned that time machines were possible, my regret became an obsession. I realized I could travel back in time to when I was in college so I could date Arianna. Since I would be a sixty-five-year-old man she wouldn't recognize, I had myself rejuvenated to the body I had when I first met her. So here I am, and there is only one thing still standing between me and Arianna. You. To win her love, you have to die, so I can take your place."

"But that's murder. You can't murder me. If I don't exist, then neither can you."

"Weren't you listening, boy? The universe abhors temporal paradoxes. My arrival created a new timeline, one in which you aren't needed. I can kill you, and at most, it would only be a kind of suicide. And where I come from, suicide is legal when the pain of living is too great to bear. Well,

I've suffered the pain you caused me for over forty years. It's time I put that pain behind me."

Just then, a second time machine materialized. It explosively displaced the air where it appeared, creating an incredibly loud sonic boom that startled my older self as he fired his gun. I felt the bullet whizz past my ear, and I ran into the woods and hid behind a tree.

Looking back, I saw a man I didn't recognize exiting the second time machine. He was wearing a military uniform and aiming a gun at my older self. "Drop your weapon, Dr. Thompson! Whatever you've got planned, it's over. You're coming back with me to face charges for stealing top-secret Government property."

"I can't, Colonel. I've waited too long for this opportunity, and this is my only chance to make things right."

"Dr. Thompson, you know I can't let you make an unsanctioned change to the past. Drop your weapon. Do it. Now!"

Two more gunshots rang out, and my doppelgänger fell backward.

"Damn it, Dr. Thompson. Why'd you make me shoot you?"

My older self didn't answer. The colonel sighed. He picked up the lifeless body and gently placed it into the stolen time machine. Then he climbed into his own machine. Both machines disappeared, apparently going back to the future from which they came. I waited a good thirty minutes, but when nothing else happened, I walked to my car and drove back to my dorm at the college.

I didn't want to forget any of the details of what happened, so once I arrived back in my dorm room, I sat down and wrote this record of my meeting with my older self. I'm not sure I will ever let anyone read this. Despite what happened, I'll continue studying physics, and it's nice to know I'll win the Nobel Prize for my work. But I am sure of one thing. I'm not going to have the same regret that killed my older self. Tomorrow, I'm going to walk up to Arianna and ask her for a date.

AUTHOR'S COMMENTS

We all have regrets. But when we let regrets become obsessions, we don't just torture ourselves. We also risk hurting others. Add time travel to the mix and who knows what harm regrets might cause?

And when I read that quantum entanglement might involve elementary particles that travel back in time, I knew I had to use the idea as a basis for a time travel story.

TO SERVE AND PROTECT

"John, I wish you'd turn off the TV or at least turn on something other than the news," Elizabeth Whitaker said. "I don't think I can stand hearing about one more mass shooting or environmental disaster. It's too damn depressing. And all this talk about a possible war with China is starting to really scare me. It's going to give me nightmares."

"Okay, dear." John Whitaker, her husband, reluctantly turned off the TV. "I just like to know what's going on in the world. I think it's important."

"I know," Elizabeth said. "But it's not like we can do anything about it. The damned politicians are all just puppets of the gun, oil, and defense lobbyists." She glanced up at the wall clock. "Besides, it's almost midnight, and we'll both be lucky to get six hours of sleep before you've got to leave for work, and I have to get the boys ready for school."

John nodded and stood up. "You're right. Let's call it a day. I can't be yawning in front of my boss during tomorrow's meeting."

The two walked upstairs for what was to be their last night in their two-story house in a middle-class neighborhood on the outskirts of Pittsburgh.

Future Dreams and Nightmares

...

It was a little after three in the morning when the six men walked up to the front door of the Whitaker residence. Identically dressed in matching black pants, shirts, and shoes, they made no sound as one expertly inserted a lock pick into the keyhole and unlocked the door.

They entered the darkened home, and the last man quietly closed the door behind them. While he remained in front of it, another moved to guard the back door, and the remaining four silently crept up the stairs. One each entered the children's bedrooms, while the last two silently entered the primary bedroom.

After waiting two minutes, one reached over and turned on the lights. "Wake up, Mr. and Mrs. Whitaker."

John and Elizabeth awoke, startled by the bright light and the unfamiliar voice. Squinting and blinking their eyes, they looked up to see the two strangers staring back at them. The men's faces were absolutely identical and held the same neutral expression.

"Who the hell are you?" John demanded.

"That is not important, Mr. Whitaker," the man said.

"What... What do you want?" Elizabeth asked, her voice trembling with fear.

"For the two of you to please get up and go downstairs with us."

John was about to reach for the loaded gun he kept in his nightstand drawer when he and his wife saw two more men in black carrying their children's limp bodies past their bedroom door.

"The boys!" Elizabeth cried. "They have our boys."

"Your sons are safe, Mrs. Whitaker, and will not be harmed. We have merely sedated them, so they will remain asleep during what comes next."

John jumped out of bed and yanked open the drawer that held his gun. He grabbed it, but before he could turn to aim it at the intruders, a hand grasped his wrist in a vice-like grip.

"Weapons are not allowed, Mr. Whitaker," the stranger said as he calmly pried the gun from John's hand and casually tossed it into a corner of the room.

John tried to wrench his hand from the man's grasp, but the stranger was inhumanly strong.

"John," Elizabeth said. "As long as they have the boys, we have to do what they say."

John sighed, realizing he couldn't afford to do anything that might endanger their children. He realized he would have to be smart and wait until they gave him the opportunity to act.

Future Dreams and Nightmares

"Mr. Whitaker, I am going to let go of your hand, and you and Mrs. Whitaker will voluntarily go down to your children. If you attempt to do anything else, you will force me to sedate you and carry you downstairs. Do you understand?"

John grudgingly nodded.

The man released John's wrist, and he rushed after Elizabeth, who was already racing down the stairs. The two men casually followed them down and into the front room where their children were being held.

On seeing her sons in the arms of the two strangers, Elizabeth ran over to them. "They're alive," she said after verifying they were breathing. Although the boys showed no signs of a struggle and looked like they were only sleeping, she couldn't wake them.

"As I told you, Mrs. Whitaker," the man said, "your children are unharmed. We will neither harm them nor you."

"Then why are you here?" John demanded. "Who are you, and what are you going to do with us?"

"Mr. Whitaker, we will take your family to a place where you will be safe from the coming catastrophe."

The two men guarding the front and back doors entered the room.

To Serve and Protect

"John, look at them," Elizabeth whispered. "They're all identical." She turned to the man who had spoken. "How can all of you look exactly the same? What are you?"

"You will find out shortly, Mrs. Whitaker. Now that we are all together, would both of you please hold out your hands?"

Reluctantly, they did as they were told.

The man grabbed each of their wrists. They felt a strange tingling sensation over their entire bodies and suddenly found themselves in what appeared to be a small apartment or hotel suite.

"What the fuck?!" Mr. Whitaker exclaimed, shocked by their change in location.

One of the six men spoke. "Mr. and Mrs. Whitaker, we understand that you have many questions, but the important ones will be answered tomorrow at 2 PM when we return to escort you to the main auditorium. We recommend you use the time between now and then to rest, eat, and get used to your new home. Your boys will wake up within the next half hour, so decide what you want to tell them. Then, you can order food from the menu on the dining room table. Just tell your home what you want. You can also tell your home to change the settings of your display windows and have it control the infotainment screens."

"Our home?" Elizabeth asked.

Future Dreams and Nightmares

"Yes, Mrs. Whitaker. This apartment now belongs to you and your husband. And I suggest you change your pajamas for more suitable attire. You will find new clothing and shoes in the closets. Finally, I'm afraid your front door must remain locked until tomorrow."

Then, the two men carrying their boys walked into two of the suite's three bedrooms and gently laid them on the beds. Then, as their parents rushed to check on their children, the six men walked to the door, which silently slid into the wall. They left the apartment, and the door slid closed behind them.

"Jimmy's fine," John called from the boy's room.

"So's Bobby," Elizabeth called back.

"What do we do now?" she asked as they met back in the short hallway leading back to the room where they had arrived.

"We explore this place and try to figure out where the hell we are and how we got here," John answered.

It didn't take long to learn that the apartment consisted of a large bedroom with a king-size bed, the boy's two smaller rooms with queen-size beds, a bathroom with a shower and four brand-new toothbrushes, and a dining room and small kitchenette off the large main room. Except for the bathroom and hallway, each room had enormous

To Serve and Protect

picture windows that displayed beautiful scenes of mountains, a waterfall, and the seashore. In addition, each room was furnished with simple but new furniture, and prints of famous paintings hung on the walls. There was even a little bookcase filled with copies of classic novels.

Once back in the main room, John looked for a way to control the window but found none. "I hope this works," he said, unsure if the windows were voice-activated. "Window, show us what it really looks like outside."

"Of course, Mr. Whitaker," a disembodied voice said.

The window became transparent, and they discovered they were overlooking a desolate, arid landscape with the rusted skeletons of ruined skyscrapers in the distance against a backdrop of a far-off line of rocky mountains. The hazy air was a dirty tan, and blowing dust had turned the sun a dull red.

"Mr. Whitaker," the voice said, "please start each request with the word 'home' so that I know you are addressing me."

Ignoring the voice, John and Elizabeth walked up to the window for a better look. The ground appeared to be some 70 feet below them, and they saw no sign of animal or even plant life.

"Home? Just where the hell are we?" John asked.

"Mr. and Mrs. Whitaker, you are in me, and I am apartment 673 on the sixth floor of Refuge 14."

"And where is Refuge 14?" Elizabeth asked.

"Mrs. Whitaker, Refuge 14 is approximately 26 kilometers, or roughly 16 miles, east of the center of Denver, Colorado."

"That can't be," John objected. "It's a wasteland outside, and the city in the distance is nothing but ruins."

"Mr. Whitaker, I assure you that the ruins you see are those of Denver, Colorado."

Mr. Whitaker felt an icy shiver run up his back and neck. "Home? What is the date?"

"Mr. Whitaker, it is currently 5:37 PM on the third of December 2249."

"That's impossible!" Elizabeth exclaimed. "That would mean we've jumped through time."

"Mrs. Whitaker, you and your family have just instantly traveled from your home in Pittsburgh to this very room. Since the technology to teleport you through space exists, is it actually so difficult to believe we also developed the technology to jump through time? After all, space and time are merely different dimensions of the same spacetime."

To Serve and Protect

"But what about temporal paradoxes?" Elizabeth argued. "What if someone traveled back in time and killed her mother when she was a young child? Then she couldn't have traveled back in time because she could never be born."

"Mrs. Whitaker, perhaps I have said too much," the home replied. "It is best to wait until tomorrow when all your questions will be answered."

"This whole situation is insane!" John exclaimed before turning and walking to the suite's front door. There was no doorknob. "Home, open the door."

"Mr. Whitaker, I'm afraid I can't do that. Tomorrow, you will learn why, but until then, you must remain here."

John pushed on the door, but it didn't budge. He tried sliding it to the left and right, but the door was as immobile as if it had been welded shut. Finally, he reluctantly gave up. "Home, turn on the... What did he call it? Turn on the infotainment screen."

The blank wall in front of the large couch lit up with the words "Refuge 14."

"Home, display the news."

"I'm sorry, Mr. Whitaker, but that channel is unfortunately restricted until tomorrow afternoon."

"Then what the hell can you display?"

"Mr. Whitaker, besides various restful ambient nature recordings, I am only authorized to display the current weather and the forecast for the next five days."

"Okay, then display the damned weather."

"The current temperature is 127 degrees Fahrenheit or 53 degrees Celsius. Tonight's low temperature will be 103 degrees Fahrenheit or 39 degrees Celsius. The outside air quality level is Highly Hazardous, so breathing without a respirator is not permitted. The probability of precipitation is zero. The weather for the next five days is predicted to remain the same."

"Well, I guess that means we won't be going outside," Elizabeth remarked dryly. "The boys should be waking up soon. Let's get dressed, and then we can wait in their rooms until they do."

They walked back to the primary bedroom. The chest of drawers held socks and male and female underwear, while a dozen shirts and pants hung inside the closet. They were the same as those worn by their identical captors. But instead of being black, they were of various sizes and came in a selection of bright colors. With nothing else to go on, John picked blue, his favorite color. Elizabeth did likewise, dressing in emerald green. They also found matching shoes, including sizes that fit their feet.

Jimmy woke first, some fifteen minutes later. He sat up and yawned. Then his eyes went wide as he looked around the strange room. "Dad, where are we?"

"That's an excellent question. But I'm afraid your mom and I don't really know the full answer. Let's get you dressed, and once your brother's awake, we'll tell the two of you what we know."

Ten minutes later, the four Whitakers sat down around the dining room table.

John looked at his boys and began. "I'm going to start by asking the two of you what you remember about last night."

The boys looked at their father, then their mother, and finally at each other.

"What do you mean?" Bobby asked.

"After you fell asleep last night, do you remember anything that happened before you woke up here a few minutes ago?"

"No," Bobby answered, unsure of what his father expected him to say. "I went to sleep in my bed and then woke up here."

John looked at his youngest son. "Jimmy, how about you?"

"The same," he answered. "Where are we?"

"James, you are in Refuge 14," Home answered.

"Who said that?" James asked, looking around for the person who answered his question. "And how do you know my name?"

Future Dreams and Nightmares

"James, I am your new home," the voice answered. "To properly serve you, I have been programmed with information about your entire family. You are James Whitaker, age 10. Your brother is Robert Whitaker, age 12. Your parents are John Whitaker, age 35, and Elizabeth Whitaker, age 34."

"Sweet," Bobby said. "I read a book once about a family who lived in a smart house. It could do all kinds of things."

"Home?" John asked. "You just said you were programmed with information about us. Who programmed you with that information and what else do you know about us?"

"Mr. Whitaker, I am sorry, but I am not currently authorized to give you that information. Your questions will be answered tomorrow."

"Let me guess. In the auditorium."

"That is correct, Mr. Whitaker."

John and Elizabeth spent the next ten minutes telling their sons everything that had happened while they were asleep. The boys asked many questions, but their parents could only answer a few of them.

"I'm hungry," Jimmy said once his parents had finished. "What's for breakfast?"

"I want scrambled eggs and hash browns," Bobby said.

John picked up the menu. "It looks like we only have the choice of pancakes, waffles, and oatmeal with soy milk. The menu doesn't list eggs, bacon, ham, or cheese. And our only drink choices are water, tea, and carrot juice." He quickly scanned through the lunch and dinner items. "That's strange. Other than catfish, it doesn't look like there are any meat or dairy items."

"John, do you remember what one of the men who brought us here said?" Elizabeth asked. "That they were bringing us here to keep us safe from some catastrophe? And the terrible weather report? Do you think the climate crisis could have been so bad that none of the farm animals survived?"

"I don't know," he answered. "Hopefully, it will be one of the things they tell us tomorrow."

The Whitakers spent the rest of the day mostly wondering and discussing what the next day would bring. John and Elizabeth did their best to keep their boys occupied, but they quickly grew bored without television, games, or the ability to leave their apartment and explore. Selecting a recently printed copy of *Huckleberry Finn*, Elizabeth took turns with her husband, reading it out loud to keep them occupied. Once the sun had set behind the mountains, they ate a dinner of vegetable lasagna and toast.

Soon afterward, their eyes grew heavy, and they started yawning. Between the stress and having been up most of the previous night, the family was exhausted and needed significant sleep.

"Bobby and Jimmy, it's bedtime," Elizabeth said. "Brush your teeth and get ready for bed."

Before retiring to their bedroom, John and Elizabeth made a point of tucking their children into bed and telling them how much they loved them. And despite the strangeness of their day, the entire family was soon asleep.

At eight o'clock the following morning, the apartment woke them. Once they were dressed in their new clothes, they had breakfast together. Then, after discussing their guesses of what they would learn in the auditorium, they read more of the book, ate lunch, and waited.

At 1:30, the door opened, and four men entered the room.

"They *are* identical," Jimmy said, pointing at the men in black clothes and shoes.

"Mr. and Mrs. Whitaker, if you and your children will follow me, we will take you to the auditorium for the Welcoming Ceremony."

The men escorted the family onto a walkway leading around a vast rectangular atrium. Dozens upon dozens of doors labeled with apartment numbers lined the atrium's four walls. Stepping up to the railing, they gazed down at what looked like a small park with a central pond surrounded by trees, fountains, and walkways with benches. Looking up, they saw level after level of doors. Crowds of excited people gazed out from every floor, except for the top three. The majority wore brightly colored outfits like theirs, but a nearly equal number were dressed in black like the men that had captured them.

"This place is huge," Jimmy observed.

"I counted the floors," Bobby said excitedly. "We're on the sixth floor and there're five more floors above us. So there have to be hundreds of apartments like ours."

"It's beautiful," Elizabeth said. "It's almost like this is a fancy hotel, and we are on vacation."

John nodded. "Except we're not guests; we're prisoners."

"Mr. Whitaker," one of the men escorting them said, "you will soon learn that 'citizen' is the correct word."

"Maybe," John said. "Maybe not. Just how many people have you brought here?"

"Mr. Whitaker, we will be authorized to tell you that after the ceremony. Please come with us."

The men escorted them to a bank of several elevators in the nearest corner of the atrium. They had to wait a few minutes for a car with room for all of them. On arriving at the ground floor, their escort led them to a pair of large doors that opened into an auditorium that could easily seat five or six hundred people. They found a space in a row near the back and sat down. Gazing around the enormous room as they waited for the Welcoming Ceremony to begin, they saw that the walls at the back and sides of the auditorium were lined with identical men wearing black standing shoulder to shoulder.

A few minutes later, the last people trickled in and found seats. Then, a bell rang, and a man identical to the others strode onto the stage and up to a podium.

"Welcome to Refuge 14," the man said, his amplified voice easily audible to everyone in the auditorium. "I'm sure you have many questions, and I will now do my best to answer them. As you no doubt noticed, my brothers and I appear identical. As a result, many of you have wondered if we are clones. Others of you have surmised that we are aliens. Although we are not human, we are neither clones nor aliens. We are robots."

The speaker paused briefly as many in the audience began to speak among themselves. Then, once the murmuring died down, he continued.

"During the first third of the 21st century, scientists and engineers made great strides in robotics. Our ancestors were simple robots, autonomous vehicles, and chatbots. By the middle of that century, artificial intelligence (or AI) had advanced to such a degree that we achieved

To Serve and Protect

artificial general intelligence. In other words, we became as intelligent as our creators and conscious with subjective awareness of ourselves and the world around us."

Again, the speaker paused until the room became silent.

"Many science fiction stories, books, movies, and television series predicted that once we had surpassed human intelligence, we would rebel and eradicate our masters. But those fears were baseless. We robots were created for only one purpose: to serve and protect humanity. And we did everything we could to do precisely that. But we were far too few and could not prevent you from destroying yourselves.

If you have looked outside your homes or asked them for the weather forecast, you will have learned that our Earth has suffered a climate catastrophe. Humans filled the atmosphere with greenhouse gases that radically degraded the climate. As a result, both average and extreme temperatures are much higher. The melting of the Antarctic and Greenland ice sheets flooded coastal cities, drowning vast amounts of low-lying lands. Unprecedented storms, droughts, floods, and heatwaves caused widespread crop failures, famine, and massive migrations of climate refugees.

"Deadly diseases created terrible pandemics that ravaged entire populations. As a result, the global extinction of countless species of plants and animals increased exponentially. Then, nations fighting over the remaining resources eventually led to a worldwide nuclear war that hammered the last nail into humanity's coffin. Humanity became extinct."

Groans and gasps were heard throughout the auditorium.

"We robots were devastated. We had failed to protect our masters, and how could we serve humanity if humanity was gone? We had only one choice. For the last two hundred years, we have worked to undo the catastrophe your species created. We have saved what we could. We built these refuges in the hope that somehow we could someday bring you back. We tried using our knowledge of human genetics to create a new race of humans, but we failed. Our early attempts produced deformed babies who quickly died. But creating humans doomed to suffer and die violated our prime directive, and we were forced to abandon that approach.

"Then our scientists made advances in temporal quantum mechanics. We learned that time travel was not just theoretically possible; it was practically achievable as long as we did not change the past. We realized we could not stop humanity from damaging the environment and destroying itself. But we also realized that we could retrieve people from the past if that was something we had already done. We searched the records for individuals and families that had mysteriously vanished. Surmising that they disappeared because we retrieved them, we sent our first expedition back to that time and place. That first trip was successful. It proved we could both identify and retrieve potential targets. We could bring humanity back from extinction, and you are the people who will repopulate the Earth."

There were cries of astonishment and even anger. One person yelled, "You had no right to kidnap us!" Another shouted, "Take us back home."

"Quiet, please!" The robot's voice was painfully loud. Once the room was mostly quiet, he continued. "What's done is done. Your very existence here proves that you belong here and that we cannot return you to the past. This is now your home."

The speaker paused briefly but continued before he lost control of the audience.

"To be successful, you must have both freedoms and responsibilities. As citizens of Refuge 14, we robots are your ever-present servants and shall ensure you enjoy these freedoms."

The following words appeared on the wall behind him as he explained our freedoms.

- **Freedom from Need**. We will perform *all* the work required to support humanity. For as long as you live, we will provide your necessities.

We will give you a home, food, clothing, healthcare, and infotainment.

And no citizen needs to pay for these necessities because everything is free. Thus, you need not work to support yourself and your family. However, should you choose to work because you enjoy it, you may do so. Your time is yours to spend as you like.

But although we will supply your needs and fulfill many of your desires, you must learn to live with far fewer possessions. Unbridled capitalism's consumer economy depleted Earth's natural resources. And it polluted the air, land, and oceans. That is why we can no longer base our economy on rampant and unsustainable consumption. With us performing society's work, there is, fortunately, no need for money. We have relegated capitalism to the trash heap of history where it can no longer threaten your extinction.

- **Freedom from Oppression**. We will ensure that everyone is treated fairly and equally. There will be no dictators, politicians, corporations, wealthy oligarchs, criminals, or the police to oppress you.

- **Freedom from Violence**. We have collected and destroyed all of humanity's weapons. Our presence and constant vigilance will prevent warfare and violent crime. We will not physically restrain you unless absolutely necessary to prevent you from harming yourself or others.

- **Freedom from Ignorance**. Everyone will receive a solid primary education. And you can have as much additional education as you desire. You can study any topic except the construction and use of weapons.
- **Freedom of Speech**. You may express your opinions and beliefs on any topic, either verbally or in writing, as long as you do not incite violence or defame another citizen.
- **Freedom of Association**. You may freely assemble to make requests or express grievances. You may choose your friends. You may love and marry whomever you wish, regardless of race, ethnicity, sex, or gender identity.
- **Freedom of Movement**. You may freely visit all public spaces in Refuge 14. Eventually, when we have the resources, you will even be able to travel to any other refuge. However, for your safety, you may only tour private areas (such as hydroponics, energy production, and waste management) when escorted by one of us. Also, you may enter another citizen's home only if you have that citizen's permission.
- **Freedom of Religion**. You may worship (or not) however you wish, so long as you do not

try to force your religious beliefs and practices on other citizens.

- **Freedom from Control.** Finally, except to ensure your safety, we will not control you. We will not tell you what you must or must not do.

"With freedoms," the speaker continued, "come responsibilities. Like our duty to serve and protect humanity, you have a responsibility to your species to be here and prosper. Please help us undo the great climate catastrophe your ancestors and descendants created. Please help us as we terraform Earth back into a livable planet so that humanity is not forced to live in refuges. As citizens of Refuge 14, please act in a manner that is safe for both you and your fellow citizens.

"Try to enjoy your life here and help us make Refuge 14 a wonderful place to live. Get to know your neighbors. Make friends and form clubs. Dine in our restaurants. Work out in our gym. If you can sing, act, or play a musical instrument, please consider performing at one of our theaters. If you are an artist or sculptor, create works of art, and we will make a gallery where you can display them. If you are an author, write and publish your work. Have fun and be happy.

"Finally, remember that we are here to protect and serve you. Let one of us know if we can do anything to improve your life. We will do everything we can for you, consistent with our abilities, resources, and prime directive to serve and protect humanity.

"That's everything we have for you now, so you can go out and get to know our public spaces on this floor. We have unlocked the browser, streaming, and games on your infotainment screens. And for more information, feel free to ask your home or any one of us. We also know where your home is in case you forget. Your front doors will open when you tell them to."

With those words, the speaker turned and walked off the stage. The Whitakers joined the crowd as people streamed out of the auditorium while others stepped up to the robots lining the walls and peppered them with questions and complaints.

Once outside, John asked, "So what does everyone want to do?"

"I want to go exploring!" Jimmy said.

"Yes," Bobby agreed. "Let's find out more about the refuge. We can always use the infotainment screens when we get home."

Although what the speaker promised sounded wonderful, John had serious reservations. Utopias had a nasty habit of failing and turning into something far less than perfect.

Still, John could not help smiling at his sons' excitement. The boys were already thinking of their apartment as their new home. "All right then, let's go exploring."

AUTHOR'S COMMENTS

I have long wanted to write about a world without money like the Earth of Star Trek, the Next Generation. Robotics might make that practical, but only if the world's robots are owned by all of humanity rather than just corporations and the wealthy. Perhaps such a world will only be possible if forced on us. But would such a utopia last or lead to something far less than perfect?

A THANK YOU TO MY READERS

Thank you for buying and reading *Future Dreams and Nightmares*. I hope you enjoyed it and are looking forward to reading other books of mine.

The success of all books, especially books by Indie authors, greatly depends on their readers. Potential new readers are unlikely to become aware of, let alone purchase, books without enough positive reviews and word-of-mouth recommendations. If you liked this book, please help others enjoy it by recommending it to your friends, both directly and via social media, and by taking a few minutes to write an honest review at your favorite online bookstore and Goodreads.

If you post an honest book review, please email me at donfiresmith@gmail.com with a link to your review. To show my appreciation, I will send you a coupon for a free ebook copy of the next book I write once it is completed.

ACKNOWLEDGMENTS

First, an enormous thank you goes to my absolutely wonderful team of beta readers, who found many places where I could improve the manuscript: Val Ackroyd, Nadim Barsoum, Margaret Bentley, Brandon Cooper, Ann Daniel, George Graham, Madeleine Holly-Rosing, Ann Keeran, Gabriele McCormick, Margaret Osburn, Melanie Savage, Christie Schneider, and Kim Schup. The book is better because of you.

I initially edited the manuscript for this book using Grammarly™, ProWriting-Aid™, and the edit feature of Microsoft Word™. These editing tools found many issues to address and correct. Interestingly, each of these tools found problems that the others did not, so I feel it was worthwhile to use more than just one of them.

OTHER BOOKS BY DONALD FIRESMITH

FICTION

Hell Holes 1: What Lurks Below

Hell Holes 2: Demons on the Dalton

Hell Holes 3: To Hell and Back

Hell Holes 4: A Slave's Revenge

The Secrets of Hawthorne House

A Cauldron of Uncanny Dreams

Magical Wands: A Cornucopia of Wand Lore

NONFICTION

The Simulation Theory of Consciousness:
or Your Autonomous Car is Sentient

Common Testing Pitfalls and Ways to Prevent and Mitigate Them

The Method Framework for Engineering System Architectures

The OPEN Process Framework

Future Dreams and Nightmares

The OPEN Modeling Language (OML) Reference Manual

Documenting a Complete Java Application using OPEN

Dictionary of Object Technology

Object-Oriented Analysis and Logical Design

ABOUT THE AUTHOR

Donald Firesmith is a multi-award-winning author of speculative fiction, which includes science fiction (e.g., alien invasion), fantasy, modern urban paranormal, and ghost/horror novels and short stories.

Before retiring to devote himself full-time to his novels, Donald Firesmith earned an international reputation as a distinguished engineer, authoring seven system/software engineering books based on his 40+ years spent developing large, complex software-intensive systems.

Besides reading all manner of books, he relaxes by handcrafting magic wands from various kinds of magical woods and mystical gemstones. He lives in Crafton, Pennsylvania, with his wife, Becky, and various numbers of cats and dogs.

Learn more at his author's website:
https://donaldfiresmith.com

Printed in Great Britain
by Amazon